The Sin Eaters

Lost Fantasies #9

LOST FANTASIES # 9 - THE SIN EATER

$5.50 per copy.

Published by Robert Weinberg, 10606 S. Central Park, Chicago, Illinois 60655.

Front cover- " Jules de Grandin" by Steve Fabian
Title page illustrations by Bob Kellough

ACKNOWLEDGMENTS

" The Sin-Eater" by G.G. Pendarves, copyright ©
1938 by Weird Tales for Weird Tales, December
1938. No record of separate renewal.

" The Withered Heart" by G.G. Pendarves, copyright ©
1939 by Weird Tales, for Weird Tales, November 1939.
No record of separate renewal.

" Dread Summons" by Paul Ernst, copyright ©
1937 by Popular Fiction Publishing Co. for
Weird Tales, November 1937. No record of
separate renewal.

" Satan's Palimpsest" by Seabury Quinn, copyright ©
1937 by Popular Fiction Publishing Co. for Weird
Tales, September 1937. Reprinted by permission
of the agent for the estate of Seabury Quinn,
Blassingame, McCauley and Wood.

" Living Buddhess" by Seabury Quinn, copyright ©
1937 by Popular Fiction Publishing Co. for
Weird Tales, November 1937. Reprinted by
permission of the agent for the estate of
Seabury Quinn, Blassingame, McCauley and Wood.

FIRST EDITION

WILDSIDE PRESS

CONTENTS

INTRODUCTION
by Robert Weinberg

Our latest LOST FANTASIES brings together five fine stories from the pages of Weird Tales. The two G.G. Pendarves stories are tales that have deserved reprinting for many years and we are pleased to be able to make them available again to fantasy fans. The two de Grandin adventures are stories that would have been included in the second series of paperback reprints of that series if such a second series had ever been done. And the Paul Ernst story, while predictable and somewhat formula, is an excellent example of what a craftsman can do with a predictable idea through fine writing. All in all, a varied and entertaining group of stories, reprinted in fac-simile from the original appearances.

Fantasy is undergoing a new revival, in both the paperback and hardcover field. Most major paper-back publishers are issuing at least one fantasy novel per month and many are coming out with several. In hardcover, there are several new series being written and horror novels and story collections are constantly among the best selling books. One could only wish that quality matched the quantity.

The problem is, as most older fans realize, that there is no market for writers to learn their craft. Beginning fantasy writers must sell their initial works to hardcover or paperback publishers. There are no magazines for them to sell stories to first - where they can learn by experimentation and hard work. It is all or nothing. There is little market for short fiction other than a variety of semi-professional magazines which by necessity are forced to pay next-to-nothing for their fiction. This sad state of affairs is best reflected in various collec-tions of " the best" fantasy which, with a total absence of logic publish new stories as part of their collection of the best of a year's work. New stories as opposed to stories which have seen print in earlier books or magazines.

As for the novels, the glut of first novels, many of them showing some promise but the strong need of an editor's blue pencil is discouraging. Originality seems to be on the wane, with one novel after another in the Tolkien tradition or the Howard style. There is no effort to do something new.

Horror novels are on the rise, with many of them making it to the best seller list. Unfortunately, to too many authors, horror seems to mean gore and unrestrained violence more than real terror. Also, there is a disturbing trend to rework and re-examine old ideas and legends instead of breaking new ground with something new and unusual. There are too many novels about modern day werewolves and vampires and not enough tales featuring new and different horrors.

What made _Weird Tales_ the " Unique Magazine" was the diversity and variety of fiction it offered. No one type of story was allowed to dominate the magazine. Perhaps some of the stories were not as successful as others, but all types were allowed and the unusual was encouraged. It was a formula which worked well for _Weird Tales_ for more than thirty years. It would work well still, if anyone would take the time to learn it.

Robert Weinberg
Editor & Publisher

"I have come ... from Hell ... to you. Hold me! Save me!"

The $\int$ in Eater

BY G. G. PENDARVES

LOOK about you! What do you think of this land where the dark experiment we shall watch takes place? This ancient haunted land of Cornwall—unfertile, unfriendly, isolated until last century from the world, even from the rest of England. Old gods, old worships, old forgotten races have died hard and lingeringly in this narrow peninsula. Cromlechs, shrines and ruined altars on many lonely hills and desolate moors still remain to remind, to suggest, with dark portents of evil.

Not long ago Black Magic darkened the thoughts and lives of men here, from Land's End to King Arthur's Seat; not long enough to purge the duchy of its evil, not long enough to drive out forces so long dominant.

7

Apparently—oh, yes—apparently only legends remain: legends useful to amuse summer visitors in company with wishing-wells, smugglers' caves, bathing-beaches, old coastguard paths, Roman forts, ancient tin mines, pilchards and clotted cream. Let it go at that. Legends!

In reality this is the story of a master scientist who dealt with human powers which few of us begin to understand. And it is always comfortable to deny the existence of what we don't understand. We demand of science improvement, discovery, bigger and better toys to play with in order that we can more easily forget the briefness of our stay in the playground itself. The science we support is obvious, spectacular, dealing only with matter, dealing with our bodies very specially that they may be bigger, better bodies so that we may stay longer to play with our toys.

But the mind of man! How convenient to forget the sciences that concern the mind of man! The majority have a touching faith in modern psychology as being a complete map to it. About as comprehensive and true a map as those of the world made in the Twelfth Century!

That's as it may be, but most readers will grant, however, the suitability of our background here in Cornwall for this, for almost any imaginable mystery. Look at the broken, towering, gloomy cliffs. They guard memories of bloodshed, violence and tragedy, of wild gales and greedy seas, of battered ships and drowning men, of wreckers more barbaric than Moorish pirates, of smugglers and press-gangs, of long centuries of struggle between man and his enemy, the sea.

On this wild coast the breaking tides boom one continuous knell—death!

And inland? Do these bare moors, this stern gray granite give you comfort?

Look closer—closer—at this old fishing-port. It is full of narrow cobbled ways, full of dark-skinned, dark-eyed fishermen, their swarming children, their hundreds of cats. This is the port of Trink. This is where we shall watch a great experiment.

We reach the great iron gates of Lamorna House—follow a shadowed drive between tall firs that moan and whisper the sea's long dirge—death! death! death!

MARK ZENNOR was dying.

He lay in his great carven bed and watched the pair of lovers with hard, merciless eyes. His young wife, Rosaina, and Stephen Lynn, his nephew, secretary and——? What else Stephen was, or would shortly be, was hidden in the dying man's thoughts.

Dying! It seemed impossible to Rosaina. She knew the doctors had given him up, said the patient was hanging on hour by hour by a miracle of will-power. She knew her husband had repeatedly affirmed this. But he seemed to her more awfully alive than ever.

*"Death, where is thy sting?
Where grave, thy victory?"*

The words flashed across her confused and terrified thoughts. Hysteria threatened. How ironical, those words, in connection with a death-bed like this! She bit her lip, closed her smarting eyes. Mark's voice stabbed her to control again. Her eyes opened to meet his sharp, cruel stare.

"Permit me to offer my sympathy. This is a most difficult role for you, my dear. Unpardonable of me to subject you to such embarrassment. It should have been so simple, so congenial a task to speed a parting guest. And an inconvenient husband at that! But *my* exit from this world? You feel something is lacking, eh? Now why?—why, Rosaina?"

Why indeed? For the life of her she couldn't formulate her deep uneasiness. Mark really was dying, there could be no question of it; all the doctors and specialists had agreed on that. A great many doctors had come and gone during the week of Mark's illness.

"It's only fair to you and Stephen that I take my departure with a good deal of publicity," he had explained. "My illness is so sudden and so unexpected that rumors might arise as to whether you two had connived at it. With all the drugs I use in my body a post-mortem would be very unconvincing."

It was remarks like this that stuck in Rosaina's mind. And the flicker of laughter in his eyes as he'd said them. At this very moment he—

8

THE SIN EATER

"You're a fool, Rosaina, but not quite such a fool as Stephen. You at least realize how little you understand my work—my art. And you are afraid. Most wise. My nephew, on the other hand—"

He turned his great head, massive and bold in outline as the carved figurehead of a ship. His dark-red hair, tonsured like a monk's, was untouched by gray in spite of his eighty years. Under a tremendous brow, his eyes glittered like quartz in strong sunlight. His nose was long, finely cut, extremely sensitive, and, in conjunction with deeply-sunken cheeks and the fine brow, would have stamped him as an intellectual and ascetic had it not been for the mouth. That was a horror, a great bar of ugly crimson across the colorless face.

Stephen Lynn did not meet his uncle's keen, stabbing glance. He sat in the glow of a cavernous red fire across the room, and though ill at ease and resentful of his uncle's characteristically unpleasant way of conducting his death-bed scene Stephen's clever, mobile face showed neither fear nor doubt.

"My nephew," pursued Mark, "is too much a man of the world, of *this* world, to share your misgivings as to the future, Rosaina.

"Imperial Caesar, dead and turned to clay,
Might stop a hole to keep the wind away.

"My widow and her wealth would stop a good-sized hole. Exactly!"

A stain of color showed in the young man's face, too pale and sharply drawn for his age and build. But Stephen was a young man of character and ambition. His uncle paid him handsomely. He'd found the resources of Lamorna library invaluable for his own private researches. And there was always Rosaina. The fact of her near and dear presence had made his difficult, often revolting work possible.

He made no reply in speech, but Mark Zennor saw the red blood in his cheeks and sniggered.

"Don't trouble to conceal your face, my boy. And your thoughts are perfectly correct, too. I am almost finished, so it's hardly worth while your taking me seriously now. I shall die before midnight."

STEPHEN frowned at the floor between his knees. He'd never got accustomed to his uncle's hateful trick of snatching the thoughts from his brain and putting them into words. He glanced across at Rosaina sitting on the far side of the great curtained bed. How nervous and strained she looked! He'd be thankful when the end came and he could take her away.

"After all, Stephen," the voice from the bed proceeded, "you owe me a good deal. You've done better for yourself here than would have been possible elsewhere. The laboratory I fitted up for your exclusive use. The lines of research I indicated. Your salary. And the beautiful widow I am so obligingly going to leave for you. All these things must be balanced against less congenial aspects of your work under my roof. In fact, I'm hoping you will not grudge a last small service—a mere trifle, I assure you."

Rosaina turned her head sharply. She recognized the note in Mark's voice with a pang of fear. He was going to ask Stephen something important—something of such importance that he thought it worth while to subdue possible opposition with a weapon that never failed him. Her own heart leaped, her pulses thrilled in response to it. Mark's voice! Against all instinct and reason, those who heard *that* note in Mark's voice had no choice but to obey.

"Don't be anxious, my beautiful Rosaina. Indeed, my child, you must not be too sad, too tragic. I assure you there is hope, there is indeed hope!"

She shivered. Hope! What did he mean by that taunt? He knew his death was the one hope she had. He knew how she loathed and feared him, how she had tried to escape. But he would not let her go. And what Mark Zennor wanted he accomplished by methods peculiar to himself. She shivered again at memory of how, in the early days of her marriage, she had tried to run away. Mark had got her back in three days by means of a dream which haunted her during her absence. A very vile little dream, if indeed that whispering obscenity which never left her day or night could be called a dream. Possibly Mark might have used a more accurate term in describing the messenger he'd sent to bring back the runaway.

"Yes, hope! You were thinking on the right lines just now, my Rosaina, when your mind ran on death. I do indeed propose to rob it of its sting. And Stephen shall help me. I leave nothing to chance, to faith. I don't live by faith—that last resort of the inferior mind. I prove everything. I *have* proved everything—everything in this extremely elementary world of ours."

"Proved everything!"

Stephen echoed the words. For a moment he actually believed the monstrous assertion. His own mind seemed to shrink and shrivel, confronted by a knowledge and intelligence brilliant as the noontide sun.

Then he was himself again, but shaken, a trifle fallen in his own esteem until he remembered a reason for his peculiar and absurd emotion. Watching by a dying man was not conducive to perfect functioning of the nerves, more especially when the dying man was his Uncle Mark. He rallied himself and smiled at Rosaina. She mustn't guess how close he'd been to sharing her own superstitious fear of this megalomaniac.

"It reassures me, Stephen, to see you smile."

Rosaina shuddered at the mad laughter in her husband's eyes.

"You appreciate this death-bed business for what it's worth, a convincing bluff for the ignorant. Objective facts of the most elementary kind are all this so-called scientific age understands. The real experiments are concerned with the spirit—with the *will*."

Will! At that ominous word Rosaina felt her blood run cold under the costly gold brocade of her gown. Mark insisted always on golden rich materials to set off her honey-gold hair and the matt pallor of her skin. The great emerald, emblem of their marriage, flashed wickedly with each nervous contraction of her hands.

"I am the only man in Europe who needs no faith. I have knowledge. I have mastered the secrets of existence."

Stephen felt completely himself now. Had it not been for Rosaina's obvious apprehensions he'd have started an argument.

"I must say I envy you," he replied. "It must be a wonderful sensation for you!"

"Sensation!"

Zennor's resonant voice gave the word an extraordinary inflection. It expressed all the mad unfathomable derision that danced in the speaker's eyes. He opened a small platinum box, took out a pellet and swallowed it.

"A drug to give that keen edge to my intellect which I find necessary in dealing with you, nephew. I am too much diverted. And I have not much longer now. My—arrangements need scrupulously exact timing. The forces I control are as implacable as they are powerful."

The younger man frowned. He'd not realized quite how mad Rosaina's husband was. He looked at her again with startled apprehension. Good heavens! Was this the sort of thing she'd had to endure? No wonder she'd talked to him so wildly. There really was something in the old devil's voice—in his eyes—something inimical he'd never felt before. What a strong horrible face his uncle had! Curious this was the first time it had seemed malevolent and spiteful. In dying, though, no doubt the face-muscles contracted. Or perhaps the shadow that lay across the bed—

He got up in some haste, stirred the fire to a blaze, threw on a log, turned up a lamp. The shadow over the bed inexplicably remained.

"It's the shadow of death, my boy! Must do the thing properly." Zennor's eyes shone incandescent as a cat's as the fire roared up the chimney. "I promised both of you I'd die within the hour, and I'll keep my word. Death. Funeral. Burial. My mortal body committed to the earth. You two can carry out the whole heathenish sequence in most irreproachable style."

ROSAINA sprang to her feet. Her panic found speech.

"Tell us, tell us quickly what you mean? What is this new trick?—this game you're playing with us?"

Zennor regarded her convulsed features with deep interest.

"You ought to have gone on the stage. Absolutely born for tragic roles! That was perfect! Perfect! I'm grateful for a moment of pure pleasure, Rosaina. It hadn't occurred to me you'd ever give me one again. I never saw you so thrillingly, vitally alive.

THE SIN EATER

Beauty! Passion! Exaltation! If a woman hasn't these she's a poor drab nuisance in the world."

Her tortured eyes looked across the bed to Stephen. He was standing by the fireplace. Irritation and some bewilderment showed on his thin tired face now. He didn't understand the awful fear that made Rosaina's face a Greek mask of horror. He didn't understand the crepitation of his own nerves. He didn't understand why his uncle, whom he'd always regarded as a man of brilliant intellect most grossly misapplied and therefore faintly contemptible, should now be inexplicably dominating, even portentous.

The vast shadowy room was very still for a spellbound minute. Huge black candles burned in wooden standards four feet high and stood in a wide semicircle at the foot of the bed. Their wax gave off a faint scent of ambergris. Three uncurtained windows showed a staring moon and hard bright stars in a sky like polished gleaming steel. Rising wind made the dark firs toss and moan about the house. A dog's long dreary howl rose.

"Stephen!"

Rosaina's voice was like the clash of cymbals.

"Stephen! Take care—ah, take care! There is danger! Mark is not dying—not dying, I tell you! It's a trap for you, my darling. Stephen! Stephen!"

Zennor's big smooth supple hands flickered in a movement so swift that Stephen couldn't then, or afterward, recall exactly what he thought he saw, whether from the deepening pall of darkness over the bed a wing fluttered, a claw-like hand leaped forth, or if . . . if it was merely an effect of smoke and flame drawn with sudden swift roar up the great chimney.

Rosaina's hands flew to her throat. She gave a choking cry and fell back in her chair. Zennor's steely gaze turned from her to Stephen.

"Hysteria. I shall be dead in another fifteen minutes in spite of her unwarrantable lack of faith in my promise. You will spare fifteen minutes to hear a dying man's request?"

The cool convincing musical voice checked Stephen. Rosaina was overwrought. She'd had the devil of a time. But now—

well, it was only decent to humor his uncle in his last moments.

"If there's anything special, Uncle Mark, anything I can do for you, of course I'll be glad to carry out instructions."

His eyes sought Rosaina. She looked a great deal more like dying than did the man on the bed. Rigid as if bound to her chair, her face, her eyes, her straining throat, every line of her body showed terror bordering on madness.

"She will recover. I shall not."

The words came from the shadow slowly, solemnly. They riveted Stephen's whole attention.

"I am listening, Uncle Mark."

"Then it is soon told. *I wish you to be my sin-eater.*"

The fantastic words meant nothing to the listener. He waited. Mark Zennor's brilliant eyes were turned toward an hourglass set in an alcove near by. Filled with blood-red sand, it was swung between supports formed by two nude figures of transparent amber glass. The thing was of exquisite workmanship wrought by a craftsman whose skill was only equaled by his obscenity.

"The last sands are running out, the last minutes of my life. Soon the glass will turn over. In the moment of its turning I intend to make the change you call death. I have planned this ever since you came here, nephew. It is no question of my eighty years, of failing powers. My brain and body are not affected by time. I learned the small secret of prolonging the life of the body here centuries ago. Oh, it was easy to produce symptoms for the doctors if you're remembering their babble! Sant's the only man who'd have guessed."

His fingers crisped in angry recollection.

"Sant! The only man who might—"

He glanced again at the hourglass and checked himself.

"I have work that can't be completed on this plane of existence. I am hampered by my body, restricted by its laws. So I shall die."

He caught and held his nephew's eye.

"I ask you only to keep vigil for one hour by my body when I am dead. And then to eat bread, to drink water, and repeat the few words written on this parchment."

11

He showed a small scroll tied with black tape and sealed. Stephen glanced at the still figure of Rosaina. How ill and queer she looked! It was difficult to think of anything else. His uncle's thick lips twitched in savage amusement.

"She hears and sees you very well. But she is—er—prevented from joining this last intimate talk between us."

"You've—you've hypnotized her!"

Stephen dashed across the room, took the girl's cold stiff hands, called her name. His frantic efforts might as well have been addressed to the chair on which she sat. He swung back to the mocking, mountainous figure on the bed.

"What have you done to her? You old devil! I'll go and call—"

"*No!*"

Stephen was held in a vise. He could neither speak nor move.

"Unless you swear to obey me, swear to be my sin-eater, Rosaina shall never wake. She shall die in trance as she is now. I can rely on Those who serve me to see to it after I am gone. You can't help her any more than you can help yourself now."

Furiously aware of sudden utter helplessness, Stephen heard Mark Zennor's voice. Its deep organ-note filled the room; its terrible music bound his soul in chains.

"Swear, Stephen Lynn! Come close. Put your hand in mine and swear!"

In spite of fiercest effort, Stephen felt himself obeying the voice, the lambent burning eyes that drew him . . . drew him . . .

He was compelled. His slow, reluctant feet moved forward, he began to cross the width of polished floor between fire and bed. It seemed like some tremendous journey. Cold, deadly conviction of loss and loneliness made those few yards of flooring beneath his feet wider than all the deserts of the world.

Rosaina and his love for her, Rosaina's stricken body close beside him, Rosaina and all their winged and shining future faded in that moment of his strange journey to Mark Zennor's bedside, faded to a small cloudy dream . . . insubstantial . . . drifting . . . drifting out of sight . . . out of mind.

Midnight approached.

The blood-red sands sank low in the hourglass, trickling through a bunch of glass grapes held by an excessively female figure into the opened mouth of an aggressively male one. When the glass swung over, the sands would flow back in a fashion as original as it was unprintable.

Stephen glanced up at the thing and back to the still figure on the bed.

Thank heaven! His hour of vigil was almost over. An hour. It seemed a lifetime since he had pledged himself, left hand in the dying man's cold strong grip, to carry out his uncle's last wish—to be his sin-eater. What a perfectly silly heathenish little ceremonial! And what peculiarly different things brought comfort to the dying! Certainly this last whim of his Uncle Mark's was outstandingly strange.

Little the dead man had ever cared about his sins! A man who refused to recognize any moral code at all, who never applied the words *good* or *evil* to conduct, who lived for experience alone—any—all experience.

His sin-eater! Fantastic notion! When last wishes had been mentioned, Stephen had imagined something far more formidable, something aimed at separating him from Rosaina. But this sin-eating business was merely a gesture—and a pitiful one considering the dead man's extraordinary intellect.

A baffling incalculable character. Sometimes he'd practiced harsh rigid asceticism, reduced his great frame to a skeleton. Sometimes he'd indulged his senses in debaucheries that ought to have killed him— and didn't! He'd used brain and body to their utmost capacity in every conceivable way.

Stephen had known all this before taking on the duties of a secretary two years ago. What he hadn't known, and still didn't believe in, was the reality of the dead man's art. That was his uncle's name for the overruling interest of his violent and checkered life. Stephen was a brilliant young man in his own particular line but he never conceived of anything that came under the heading of occult as being more than the rankest imagination. And imagination, he reasoned, belonged to poets and children in its better manifestations, and to drugfiends and the morally and mentally deficient in its worse ones.

When a man died, argued Stephen, he utterly ceased to be, save as a memory. Death—death of the body was the end of a man as a separate individual. His work alone survived.

His uncle's work! Stephen reflected on it as represented by the many books that bore Mark Zennor's name. He'd read some of them, a few that were written in English and dealt with scientific subjects. He'd been taken out of his depth and had never tackled the more recondite in German and French. There were books on philosophy in Chinese, Sanskrit, and Hebrew. There were books on music equally beyond his comprehension. He'd tried a volume of poetry once but decided that all the Turkish baths in the world wouldn't make him feel clean after such literary explorations as these.

However, there was one book in the Lamorna library which he had been forced to know from cover to cover. He had made its black linen covers himself and printed every word of the text between them. It was not published, not publishable. It had been his first and most unpleasant task as his uncle's secretary to print this book on the private press that Zennor owned. A short book and a damnable one. The author's references to past vile experiences and experiments, and to others even more monstrous which he intended to carry out, haunted Stephen for months. To his clear young mind such revelations of immense research and familiarity with unspeakable beliefs and practices were lewd expressions of insanity, the excesses of a megalomaniac whose ambitions rivaled Lucifer's.

Finally, however, he grew callous. Profound disbelief enabled him to do his daily work with the detachment of a machine. He ceased even to wonder why his uncle had wasted time and his amazing intellectual powers over such insane and filthy nonsense.

"Yes, filthy nonsense!"

He repeated the words aloud. He was beginning to feel the necessity of reassurance. This vigil was getting on his nerves. Something was wrong with the lamp—it needed refilling, perhaps. His uncle had insisted on lamps and costly special oil for them that made the whole house reek. Tonight the lamp and the fire too—what was

wrong?—everything seemed on the jump. Shadows. Beastly what queer imitations of life a shadow could give! Shadows—in that foul little book—they were said to be—

He thrust back persistent words and images, and glanced toward the bed. The old man looked extraordinary. His arms and hands lay naturally by his side, the fingers crisped a little in the characteristic way they had in life. His eyes were open.

"Don't close my eyes, remember, Stephen!" he had commanded. "I want to watch you perform the ceremony."

And, although Stephen would have preferred to close those merciless bright eyes, he had given his word and could not bring himself to break it. He tried however, to be mocking at his obedience, to be watching, waiting . . . waiting . . .

He attempted once more to reason about the thing.

"It's merely reflex action. The old man died believing in all his sticky little devil-worshipping ideas. He died happy in the thought that he was pushing all the results of his highly colored life on to my shoulders and went off believing this sin-eating business would square his accounts. That explains the peculiar expression in his eyes. And that half-smile!"

He frowned, stared.

"It certainly seems more pronounced. Probably it's those drugs he poured into himself to keep going as long as he wanted. When the rigor passes his muscles will relax. Nasty look on a dead face though—very nasty. Still it's perfectly explainable—perfectly!"

He wrenched his gaze from those fixed sightless eyes. Sightless! It was hard to believe they really were that.

"He knew what he was about when he made me promise not to close them. Damned if the old devil's not at his old games even now he's dead. Trying to hypnotize me."

He moved restlessly, tried to laugh. The face of the dead expressed considerably more amusement than did his own; yet remembrance of this trick of his uncle's brought relief to the watcher. Hypnotism! That was it. That covered everything, especially the strange sensations he'd had just before his Uncle Mark had died. Idiotic to have laid himself open to it—to have let imagination ride him so completely. Thanks be! It had passed off almost at once.

Probably Rosaina's collapse had unnerved him, made him susceptible to suggestion. It was the very first time his uncle had ever caught *him* napping. His self-congratulation was unclouded by suspicion of design in this fact.

Rosaina! He looked at her. Still as a statue, white, frozen. Nothing he said or did could wake her.

"When you've fulfilled your promise, Stephen! She won't wake until then," Zennor had repeated. "Not until the hour is up and you've become my sin-eater."

Somehow he felt less concerned about her now—the strained white face, the terror-filled eyes, the slender limbs held as if in bonds! Hypnotized. He felt a faint contempt for the weakness that made her so easy a victim, even a sort of respect for the dominance of a will that could, even after death, exert its influence. Anyhow, if she were in a trance she felt nothing. No use his agonizing over her. Not long now to wait.

A FAINT whirring of machinery drew his glance to the hourglass. Its last grains had run out. Chimes of midnight sounded from some deep-toned village clock. Noiselessly, smoothly, the big hourglass turned in its half-circle.

He got to his feet, stood beside the dead body. At last he'd get the thing over and done with.

The first red grains ran back as he stretched out a hand toward the bared breast of the corpse. Those eyes! The light in them still. Surely—surely the dull fire couldn't strike that gleam in them? No, of course not. It was those infernal candles at the foot of the bed. Probably the wax contained some filthy ingredient that was affecting his eyes. Nothing his Uncle Mark had used was normal or natural. He was forever experimenting on his own senses and on other people's. The whole house ought to be burned down. Fire was the only purge for so much dangerous rubbish. That book in the library—everything suggestive, indecent. Yes, fire was the proper

cure. He was so furious, so humiliated by the repugnant fear he felt of touching the corpse that he suddenly shouted at it:

"I'd like to burn the house down and you in it!"

Naturally there was no reply. Or was there? Didn't the dead man's grinning lips draw back a trifle further? Didn't the fixed eyeballs roll slightly in their sockets to meet his frantic angry gaze?

He cursed himself for a fool. A fool to have promised to carry out this fantastic post-mortem charade. A fool not to break his promise now. And fool most of all to get the wind up like this if he *was* going to do it.

He forced himself to take the parchment roll from under the dead man's hand.

He broke its black seal, unwound the tape, opened out the crackling sheet. His face darkened as he read the strong black lettering. This thing that seemed so childish and superstitious an hour ago began to assume a new aspect in its fulfilment. And for this, Stephen cursed his imagination now, rather than his lack of it in the first place.

Consulting the parchment from minute to minute he began to obey the directions written there.

"Take up the wafer that is in the mazar-bowl," he read. "Mazar? I suppose he means black-cherry wood."

Yes, there was the small wooden bowl on a table beside the bed. He took out of it a wafer whose smooth black surface was pricked in a deadly device he failed to understand. His fingers, colder than the dead flesh he touched, placed the wafer on the bared breast of the corpse.

Another, smaller bowl stood filled with water. And this also he put on the dead man's breast.

Then, turning to the table again, he dipped his trembling fingers into a handful of salt around which five minute black candles burned in a circle. Their tiny flames licked up fiercely as his hand was outstretched above them. Pain set his whole body on fire. He stood rigid, agonized. Suddenly the burning ceased. Only in his brain a strange sense of heat remained as if the fiery ordeal had left a spark upon the altar of his mind.

THE SIN EATER

The salt he had taken up he now sprinkled upon the wafer and into the water. Once again he consulted the written words, put out an obedient hand, let it fall with a groan.

"No! No!" he muttered. "I don't like this business. It's—there's something I don't like about it! I believe he's—"

Against his will he looked up, caught the fixed dead eyes that seemed so piercingly to watch him, and again he felt a sense of utter powerlessness. Again, as when he first agreed to be his uncle's sin-eater, his resolution fatally relaxed. The fire in his brain dissolved the half-formed premonition of his danger.

Before the hard cold glitter in the dead man's eyes his own fell. He raised the bowl of water and held it out with stiffly extended arms toward the corpse. His hoarse strained voice came haltingly:

"I drink this water, with salt that can compel, that your sins may be washed from your soul. Let them flow—as this water—from you to me. I receive the great darkness of your sins. I give the light of my soul that your own may walk in it forever."

He shuddered violently as he turned, bowl in hand, to each of the four corners of the room, repeating the form of words each time. Then, putting the water to his lips he drained it and tossed the bowl away.

And now he knew no trick of candle or firelight had set that flame of wicked malice dancing in the eyes that held his own, or brought those capering shadows all about him. The fire within his brain worked like madness. He was part of all this now. He loved as much as loathed it. He desired as greatly as he feared to share the dead man's secret power.

He took up the wafer, turned again to each corner of the darkening room to repeat the written formula. Now his voice rose loud and defiant as he faced the corpse:

"Mark Zennor, with this bread and the salt that has power to seal my vow, I eat your sins. Give me the burden of them. I take their weight on my soul. I, your sin-eater, give my soul's rest for yours eternally."

He put the wafer in his mouth. It crumbled to salt dust on his tongue. As he swallowed it he was aware that the flame of life within him was rising higher—higher—higher. And, with its soaring, towering, leaping life, he seemed to touch the stars. Then, with awful downward plunge, he sank—swift—swooning—down to thunderous abysmal dark. . . .

"STEPHEN! Stephen!"

He roused himself. Rosaina was kneeling by his side where he lay on the floor. Her arms were about him. Her tears fell on his face. He got up, drawing her also to her feet, and looked down at her tragic face. He felt as though he'd been under the sea, submerged, almost drowned. His fears, his pain, the madness in his brain were washed away.

Rosaina held him with desperate convulsive pressure. He felt the wild beating of her heart against his breast. She couldn't speak. His low murmured words of love seemed to increase her dreadful shuddering agitation.

At last her sobbing breath was stilled, and she leaned against him in utter exhaustion as he stroked her golden shining hair.

"Darling! Dearest!" he whispered. "He's gone at last, left us free, you and me! You and me, my own! Rose! My golden lovely Rose! Love me, love me and forget the rest."

She didn't move or speak. Once she turned to kiss the fingers that rested on her hair, and the cold pressure of her lips startled him—her clasp, her kiss were so despairing. Then she cried out again:

"Stephen! Stephen! *Stephen!*"

"Darling! I am here—holding you—close—close. Why do you call as if I were leaving you?"

"Stephen! You are—you are leaving me!"

She pushed him away, stood with white tragic face and haunted eyes.

"Oh, Stephen, my dear!—my dear! Don't you understand at all what you have done?"

"You mean that barbaric little ceremony? Dearest, you simply can't believe there's anything in that! You might as well believe in ghosts and witches and devils—or—or anything," he finished lamely.

"I do believe in devils. He was a devil—served by devils. Didn't you see what held me bound this past hour, Stephen? Didn't you *see?"*

15

"The old man hypnotized you. I tried to wake you up—I tried repeatedly."

"You saw nothing—felt nothing when you touched me? Oh, it's come, it's come at last—our punishment for loving. How fast he's got you now! He'll drag you down to hell—down to hell."

She went close to him again, looked up into his frowning bewildered face.

"His sin-eater. His sins. Have you any idea what Mark's sins were? No! How could you—when even I—although I can't sleep for remembering, for remembering—even I can only guess at—"

Her face grew ashen but she moved back from his imploring arms.

"Wait, wait, Stephen darling! Oh, try to understand—try to believe me. It was real, that ceremony of the sin-eater. You have taken Mark's sins from him."

"You really believe that?" His tone was the more emphatic for a cold creeping doubt that chilled him now. "Darling, you can't be so medieval and superstitious as that!"

"I know, I know I'm right," she urged. "You're in hideous danger. Oh, if you believed me even now it might be possible to—"

She broke off, seized his hands and pressed them to her breast.

"Stephen! Stephen! Of course, I remember now what he said to me about Mark's illness, and that I must tell him if— Come quickly, quickly! We'll ask him to help you."

She clasped him in an agony of relief.

"Mr. Sant—don't you remember?— don't you remember he said Mark was not ill? He promised to return before any crisis arose if he could."

"No, I forget all about it. But he'd think me a fool to go to him with this tale."

"Uncle Mark was mad and you can be sure Sant knew it. He's the most celebrated alienist in Europe. Sant would count me as a patient if he thought I believed this. What can it signify—a few silly words gabbled over a dead body? Look here, Rosaina, let's get out of this room and talk somewhere else; even the sight of his corpse—"

She glanced over her shoulder as they went, hand in hand, to the door. Her loud cry seemed to the man to come from his own lips as he turned and stared also at the bed.

"Look! Look! Ah-h-h! Look at him now!"

He dropped her hand, strode to the cavernous bed. The face of the corpse was the face of one utterly at peace. Its bright staring eyes were closed, its lips gravely folded, every line that lust and pride had deeply stamped was smoothed away.

It was the face of one whose soul had found its rest.

Rosaina pressed close to Stephen. She stood staring . . . staring. . . . Her white trembling lips whispered over and over and over:

"You are his sin-eater—his sin-eater— his sin-eater You have taken the evil from him."

They turned to look at each other. Her eyes searched his in frantic love and agony, dreading to see in them what he had taken from the dead. He returned her look. Faint impatience pricked him. He'd had enough melodrama for one night, he felt. Rosaina was—what had his Uncle Mark once said of an Arab woman he'd bought in Touggourt? Oh, yes! "Zobeide, my dear nephew, was a—"

He pulled himself up. Good heavens! What had brought that lewd story to his mind—and in connection with Rosaina? He turned in horrified contrition.

"Dearest, you must come away. This place reeks of him and his beastliness."

"OH, YES, please! Yes, we'll come at once. No, not here! I can't talk to you in his house."

Sant put down the telephone receiver, stood gazing at it. His mind was roused to extraordinary activity. His memory was gathering up facts, proofs, experience from the immense field of his knowledge. The whole situation was changed now.

The great tawny Persian cat, lying with head sunk between straightly extended fore-paws, felt a break in the continuity of his peace. He looked up, gave a small inquiring trill of protest. His master picked him up and tucked the satin head beneath his own chin.

"Hároon Er-Rasheed, my old friend, it's

bad news—the worst possible news! Mark Zennor is dead."

He held the cat so that he might look into his benevolent peaceful face. The animal rubbed a cold friendly nose against his own.

"Oh, yes, I know I'm clever, my dear. But so is he, most infernally so, and if he's dead it's because he didn't wish to remain alive. For the moment I can't fathom his reasons—that is what we've got to discover."

Hároon Er-Rasheed burrowed his muzzle into the palm of Sant's hand and gurgled consolation.

"Well, I'm glad you believe in me so utterly. It all helps. But we must think—we must think."

With the gentle deliberation approved by that nervously constituted aristocrat he put the big cat down. Turning to his bookshelves he took out a battered volume entitled *The Human Will*. His visitors could not be here immediately, for his house was fairly inaccessible from Trink Village and the motor-road made a very long detour.

As this is the story of Zennor's death and of certain events immediately consequent on that crisis, it would be tedious to go back in any detail into circumstances of how and when these two men had previously come into conflict. The affairs were too elaborate, a great many other people were involved in them, and they had never been in the nature of man-to-man duels. Rather, Sant had interfered, very quietly, very circumspectly on a number of occasions in order to frustrate some of Zennor's ripest and most deadly plans.

By the time a rapid muffled knocking sounded at his front door, Sant had traveled a long journey in his thoughts. His immense power of concentration had marshaled his every encounter with Zennor and criticized each anew. In the light of his last dramatic move, everything Zennor had done or not done assumed less or more importance.

"Yes," reflected Sant aloud, as he rose to let in his visitors. "His death is a retreat in one sense, but it means that he has fallen back on some superior vantage-ground. My task is to discover what it is."

The welcoming light which, from the vestibule of his house, shone like a little star on the lonely hillside, showed Rosaina and Stephen to Sant as he opened his door to them.

Both were changed. He knew that instantly. It was a new and different quality of fear that now whitened the girl's face, aging and withering her inexpressibly. In Stephen's keen alertness there was now an edge of antagonism. At first faint pattern of the dead man's plan began to take shape in Sant's mind.

He led them in to his warm fire, and it did not surprise him to see his cat pressing up against the door as he opened it, but as the creature shot past his legs and away, ears flattened back, tail stiffened in angry fright, the pattern of Sant's thoughts was stamped a trifle more clearly. His eyes took on the gray remoteness of a winter sea, always a sign of intense mental preoccupation with him. He didn't, however, communicate his thoughts, but merely listened to their story and put extremely pertinent questions.

"About that one special book you recollected when Zennor had died and you were keeping vigil by him. It seems to me very important. I must get hold of that book you printed."

"I suppose it would be a good idea." Stephen felt a peculiar reluctance all of a sudden to part with that black-bound book. "I'll see if I can find it for you."

"Thanks. Tomorrow morning, then."

Stephen was astonished at his own stab of furious anger. He was an even-tempered man and, although he was roused at rare intervals, it took a great deal to make him angry. Also, when that happened, he always felt cold as a block of ice. Never in his life before had he experienced such fiery murderous hate as flared up in him now.

SANT pretended not to see the vivid, if very fleeting, change in the other's face.

A strong revulsion of feeling seized the younger man. "Yes," he begged, "do come and take the thing away. I can't bear to remember I printed it, helped to perpetuate such foulness. It's coming back to me as we talk what it was all about, at least so far as I understood it. When I was working on

17

it I was convinced Rosaina was somehow concerned—the human sacrifice—but there were a good many sacrifices mentioned, and she couldn't have been the same 'golden woman' who died in Persia thousands of years B. C., or a Libyan princess in the time of Alexander the Great, or a slave in A. D. 50! And yet the book—"

Sant's blank calm face effectually concealed his thoughts.

"Yes. Do go on," he encouraged; "this is all most relevant."

"Of course," confessed Stephen, "most of it was gibberish to me. Uncle Mark claimed to have been reincarnated over and over again. He had to find something—or someone to complete a Triad—a mystic perfect Triad. It had to be three who were bound each to the other in some mysterious way. Then he could offer his last sacrifice through the medium of the Triple Link. His great object seemed to be the possession of a Key—"

"The Key of Thoth?"

"Yes. That's what he was after—the Key of Thoth " He met Sant's grave eyes. "It's all pretty much of a jumble in my mind. I didn't understand one word in a hundred. But I do remember that he'd got to have some special sort of co-operation for his sacrifice."

"Stephen! What else—what else?"

Rosaina's voice was sharp with anxiety.

He looked at her rather vacantly, his brows drew together, he ruffled his thick brown hair. "It was fairly evident that he felt he'd got to the end of his search. There was a lot about his High Priest and the bond of blood to seal his bargain."

Sant's eyes were very cold, very remote. "I see." He looked intently at the other man.

"Damned if you do!" blazed Stephen suddenly. "It was my uncle's great secret, the goal of all he'd ever done or thought or lived for! No one—no one ever so much as guessed at his tremendous success—at the things he'd discovered."

"Stephen!"

Rosaina's cry brought him to himself. She shrank from his touch, turned to Sant with unmistakable appeal.

"He's worn out—as you are." Sant's voice was stern now. "You mustn't show

fear, Rosaina, you mustn't feel fear! It will injure him. If your love has any depth and reality you've got to help him. You can't leave him now."

"Leave him?" stammered the girl.

"Certainly. You left him when you turned to me then. Now listen to me, both of you!"

He looked into Stephen's dark eyes. Anger made them glitter. His thin face seemed a trifle squarer, his lips a trifle fuller.

The rough dark hair took a red gleam from the firelight.

"Stephen," Sant put a hand on the other's twitching one, "you're afraid too and you're giving ground to the enemy. It's no use keeping up any sort of pretense about this; we must work together, it's our wills against—the dead!"

"His sin-eater. I am his sin-eater."

Stephen spoke, not in horror so much as in warning and reminder.

"You were ignorant and foolish. You let Zennor trick you once—are you going to let him go on doing it, Stephen Lynn?"

The other got hastily to his feet, held out his hand.

"No!—no! I'm not! No, I'm all right again now and I'll fight him until I die."

"And that won't do, either." Sant gripped him strongly. "You've got to live. You've got to find out how to free yourself."

He turned to Rosaina.

"I won't disturb my housekeeper so late —or so early! It's almost three o'clock in the morning. You shall have my room. There aren't any others ready. Stephen will do very well down here by the fire. I must go to Lamorna House at once."

He spoke with eyes on Stephen's face, saw gratitude and relief suddenly sharpen to suspicion.

Some sort of struggle was going on in the young man's mind. Sant went off with Rosaina, and returned to find Stephen in hat and coat.

"It might be better if I went back with you, after all. You can—" he hesitated. "Oh—if—of course, if you prefer—no, I'll come! You can keep an eye on me then."

His companion regarded him with absorbed attention.

"Don't you mean you want to keep an eye

on me?" he corrected. "Come if you will, by all means."

Again the younger man hesitated, then spoke in slow sulky tones.

"It would be better. The servants would think it queer if Rosaina and I were both here and you in possession at Lamorna House. Uncle Mark left like that!"

"Of course," Sant heartily concurred. "We'll go together."

THEY found Lamorna House abominably quiet—a challenging sinister quiet that met them on the threshold with all the force of swarming invisible assailants in possession of a stronghold. As they went through the hall and up the broad stairs, shadows seemed to peer and watch, to keep guard over the dead.

In the chamber of death they found the tall black candles still burning steadily at the foot of the bed. The head of the corpse lay deeply sunk into the pillows. On its face a yet profounder calm had settled. Sant looked down in silence. He hid his deep disquiet from Stephen, standing beside him; but, turning sharply, he surprised a strange smile dawning in the young man's dark eyes, a smile that spread as Sant watched it—loosening the fine curve of the mouth, aging and coarsening the eager face.

He faced the corpse and spoke a few rapid words under his breath. For a moment the look of infinite calm on Mark Zennor's face seemed to break and alter—as the surface of smooth water is ruffled by a sudden angry gust of wind.

But it was Stephen who answered Sant's words. What he said was unintelligible to himself—the words rushed from between his lips—his hands clenched—his whole body stiffened. Then, under the penetrating steady look with which Sant met his outburst he drew back. His taut muscles slackened. He looked almost stupidly bewildered.

"Sorry! Did you say anything? I felt dizzy all of a sudden."

"I didn't know you spoke Arabic!"

"Arabic!" echoed Stephen. "Why, I don't speak it—don't understand a word of it. What makes you say so?"

"Only that you cursed me very competently in that tongue just now."

Stephen's bewildered frown deepened to a scowl. "You seem as much off your balance as Rosaina. I've never spoken a word of Arabic in my life."

"Forgive me!" Sant put a hand on his arm. "I'm not playing tricks on you—it is *he* who is doing that. I wanted to prove something and I've done so. Come away. This empty shell he's left—everything here reeks of him—tainted—poisonous! Come, Stephen!"

Outside the room, Sant locked the door and pocketed the key. Instantly his companion's eyes blazed with fury, but it died down and faded at the older man's friendly smile and touch.

"Look here, Sant, I can't stand this, I'm all in a fog—can't seem to get a grip on myself. Can you give me something to make me sleep? If I could sleep, forget the last few hours, I might—"

"The very best thing," agreed the other.

THEY went downstairs again. In his own private study, Stephen switched on an electric radiator and produced drinks. An hour later he was sleeping heavily, stretched out in an easy-chair. Sant made for the library; he knew he must get hold of Mark Zennor's book before he was prevented.

He found it at last, sat down at a desk, and began to examine it. He read on and on. Dawn crept up to the tall, uncurtained windows. Warmth of the rising sun touched his cheek as he sat, fell on the printed page before him.

He got to his feet abruptly and flung up the nearest window, thrust out his head to breathe deeply of the keen salt air from the Atlantic. In the east a streak of yellow kindled behind glimmering ghostly bare trees. Ah! How good the sharp sweet air—the untainted dawn! How cleansing after the abominable pages of Zennor's book! He leaned against the window-frame, half closed his eyes, surrendered his tired mind and body to the spell.

A robin warned him. Young and bold and hungry, it fluttered to the broad sill on which his hand rested.

Cheep! Cheep! Cheep! *Cheep!*

Sant's eyelids lifted. He caught sight of a shadow on a side-pane of the bay window and turned in time to snatch up the open book. Stephen stood beside the desk, a queer stiff automatic figure, his eyes wide open but glazed with sleep. As the book was withdrawn his lips drew back in a savage grimace and a blaze of vivid hate shone through the dreaming dark eyes. The hand outstretched to pick up the book drew back with crisping crooked fingers like the talons of a bird of prey.

Sant leaned forward, looking deep into the black fixed eyes of the sleepwalker.

"No, Mark Zennor—not yet! I stand between you and this man you have betrayed. I fight for Stephen Lynn—for his body and for his soul."

Again hate leaped like white fire in the fixed eyes, and for a moment the mask of Stephen's face quivered, altered, expanded to hideous semblance of the dead.

Sant drew closer, put all his will into repulsing the assault. "Not yet," he repeated. "You dare not take possession of this human body now. The four hands of Adda Nari still hold the four elements from your grasp. You are not yet wholly freed from the Wheel. The laws of human life still bind and limit you."

Fiery hate died on blankness in the eyes opposite his own. He blew lightly in the set young face.

"Wake, my dear boy—wake!"

Stephen was bewildered, annoyed, and very tired.

"What's it all about? Sleep-walking! Never done that before. Heavens! What a beastly draft!"

He slammed down the open window against the still twittering robin and rang a bell.

"Those lazy good-for-nothing servants! Snoring away upstairs. They can jolly well come down and do their bit. I'll have enough on my hands now with funeral arrangements and all the rest of it."

He looked far more exhausted than before he'd slept.

"What were you working at? That book of my uncle's—eugh! Better burn it—burn the whole library—everything!"

"Yes, I agree, but not until I've come to the end of the trail I'm following; not until I know how strong a link he made to bind you to him."

"That sin-eating charade?" Stephen's look was derisive. "Y'know we all got the wind up pretty badly last night. No man could believe in such mumb-jumbo—not now, in broad daylight. Last night was different. After watching Uncle Mark all those hours —and he was a—well, he's gone now, no need to dissect his unpleasant character more than necessary. Anyhow last night's over and done with! As to the rest—"

"You mean you no longer feel in any danger?"

"Danger? No, except of making a fool of myself. Last night he hypnotized Rosaina and I believe he put some sort of a 'come hither' on me too. Making the most of his last hours I suppose. I don't want to think of, or talk about, or remember last night any more."

"Perfectly natural and normal, but unfortunately your attitude gives Mark Zennor a clear field."

"What—with me!"

Stephen stared, then burst into a laugh. Sounds of steps in the hall interrupted him.

"One of the Seven Sleepers at last—butler probably," he went on. "Better go and tell him about Uncle Mark. He'll want to warn the maids and trot round pulling down blinds, etc. Servants adore deaths and funerals and all the gloom and wreaths and hushed voices and all the rest of it. There won't be tears, at least. No one in the wide world could regret Uncle Mark's death. There's the telephone, that'll be Rosaina —hope she slept better than I did, poor darling!"

I T WAS after the funeral that Sant missed Stephen.

"I can drive the car, of course," he told Rosaina as he tucked a rug about her knees. "But—"

She gave a shiver, nor was it the keen north-east wind that chilled her.

"We can't wait here in the churchyard for him. Let's go back."

A crackling log-fire and Sant's big yellow cat gave them welcome. Rosaina sank to a chair by the leaping flames and tossed her hat on the rug. She'd cast aside all the rich flaunting golds that Mark had insisted on, and in a dark tweed suit she looked less sophisticated and considerably more tired and fragile.

Hároon Er-Rasheed inspected her hat

with deep interest and a running commentary of sounds peculiar to himself, then leaped to her knee.

Sant smiled down on them both. "Not much of you visible now. I must see that Zennor's book is safe before looking for Stephen."

He crossed over to a bookcase and pulled out from behind a row of dusty folios a box clamped with silver, unlocked it with a key on a bunch in his pocket.

The box was empty!

"Gone! Stephen evidently made straight for it. It had a preface with elaborate detailed instructions for reaching the hidden entrance to a vault or crypt beneath Lamorna House—Zennor had converted it into a sort of chapel."

She stared up at him.

"The book! Instructions! D'you think Stephen's gone down to the horrible place?"

"Sure of it. He's been trying to do it ever since Zennor's death. I dogged him like his own shadow—he'd no chance until this afternoon. I saw him slip away from the graveside, but I couldn't run after him then.

"I've made a copy of those instructions." He put a hand into his breast-pocket and drew out a few thin crackling sheets from a case. "Impossible to find the place without this key. I'll have to follow at once."

"I must come too. Yes!—yes!" she got to her feet impetuously. "I can't wait here alone. You don't know what horrible thoughts I have."

"Believe me, I do know, but I ask you to stay. The danger is acute for all three of us, most of all for Stephen. For his sake I must go alone. I'm not powerful enough to give you protection if sudden attack came. If you hinder me or distract me and I fail—you and he are also lost, remember."

She met his eyes bravely.

"You're very clever, and very strong. I believe in you with all my heart. And I'll do my best to—to believe in myself too. But bring Stephen back to me! Oh, bring him back!"

"**B**RING Stephen back to me!" An hour later her passionate appeal echoed in Sant's ears as if Rosaina's strained white face still looked into his, while eyes and lips implored, "Oh, bring him back to me!"

On the threshold of a vast and vaulted chapel he stood cold and stiff as the carven monstrosities within it, his eyes fixed on a great altar that faced the entrance. Before the altar a man was standing—a man who elaborately genuflected and abased himself. The man was Stephen Lynn.

Sant, who knew the value and the meaning of each gesture, knew also that he was too late to interfere.

"It would kill him outright now," he murmured; "he's in trance. Zennor's taken complete control. He means to strike at once without giving me time to prepare. Yet the Universal Agent turns to its ebb! He's broken his Rule. He means to sacrifice before his Hour."

He took a few steps into the heavy perfumed gloom. What light there was beat down upon the altar-steps, above which a great metal globe hung, suspended in mid-air by magnetic force, a globe that received long shafts of light from concealed sources and gave them off again in dazzling hypnotic points of fire.

Sant carefully avoided raising his eyes. As carefully he moved forward, choosing his steps over the bizarre mosaic of the marble floor. He knew the deadly trap of the symbolic tree whose reversed branches spread under his feet. He knew what dark magic lent iridescent gleam to the peacocks set within their topaz circles. His lips murmured the Words and a Word as he trod between the stippled ochreous coils of two serpents intertwined. His hands moved in strange rapid gestures as he followed a narrow track of alternating black and yellow tiles, setting each foot on the black, advancing with a swaying balance of a tight-rope walker.

And now he halted. On the chapel pavement before him glowed a full moon, red, ominous as spilt blood. He anxiously examined it. If the moon revealed— Yes! So faint that only an initiate might discern its awful significance, an ovoid luminous shadow moved within the confines of its own circumference, vaporous, restless, potent, dread symbol—the Orphean Egg.

Sant waited, watched a curl of bluish mist rise from the full moon's strange matrix, stood like a stone as it curled about his feet, his knees, his body, his stiffly erect head. Only with his will might he control this force—creator and destroyer before the earth was formed. Behind the dreadful veil that hung about him, his face showed the grimness of the ordeal. Vapor swirled and eddied swifter, denser every moment. Sant knew the pains of death, the pangs of rebirth, but he endured, and at last stood free.

Back to its living source the vapor sank as he moved forward to the lowest altar-step. He had received a baptism, and nothing in this place, dedicated to evil, might harm him in this hour.

He looked up instantly at the altar. The spare young figure knelt in rigid stillness now and every line expressed tense prodigious effort of concentration. A voice continuously rose and fell, but not Stephen's voice—the timbre was fuller and more richly modulated, a trained and powerful instrument whose deep notes held the sound of far-off stormy seas.

It was Mark Zennor's voice that rose and fell—rose and fell in magic compelling cadences! Zennor calling on his dark gods, reiterating his impious vows, drawing to his service a vast army of the damned.

Velvet-shod, Sant moved another step upward. And now he blotted out his own personality that it might make no impingement on the etheric waves of evil which the worshipper was drawing to himself. On all sides he felt strong pressure of occult power —subservient, dominated by the man at the altar above him.

"Bring him back to me!"

The words thrilled through his brain, for he could not obey them now. This man kneeling by the great Stone of Sacrifice was Stephen Lynn's human habitation merely. Within it, controlling, drilling an unaccustomed body to its ritual, was Mark Zennor's proud satanic brilliant mind.

"Bring Stephen back to me!"

Impossible now. Zennor had long ago too thoroughly prepared his ground, too completely trapped his victim from the first moment of their contact. He listened intently. The words rapped out firmer, quicker, more peremptory now. The climax approached.

The great chapel, circular in shape, had walls that rose curving, darkly luminous, satin-smooth as the petals of a vast black tulip, to meet a vaulted roof—their polished surface broken by squat archways behind which darkness lay like a crouching beast of prey.

Above the huge slab of the altar-stone was a reredos of red alabaster, a screen some thirty feet by ten. It was powerfully illumined from behind, so that its carving stood out in bold relief and a trick in the lighting gave a sinister effect of constant movement.

This screen was a vivid presentment of a human sacrifice. Bound on the stone-altar, a woman appeared to writhe and quiver. Her long bright hair rippled down to a deep trough about the altar-base. Into this same trough trickled a thin dark stream of blood from a knife which pierced the victim's body. About the altar stood tall candles whose flames danced in frenzy.

And behind the candles' flare and flicker, at each of the four corners of the altar, a veiled figure towered. Menacing, gigantic, these figures were the only immovable objects on the screen, and they achieved by their fateful stillness—in contrast with the surge and movement of all else in the picture—an effect of final inescapable doom. Dark crescent moons poised above each veiled head of these four attendant genii bearing Hebrew characters which read— EARTH. WINTER. NIGHT. DEATH.

And now Sant saw the black-clad figure —the body of Stephen Lynn, torn and wrenched, trembling from head to foot in diabolic ecstasy, arms flung wide, head bent backward so that light from the suspended globe beat full and fiercely down upon the upturned face. Louder—louder rang the great triumphant organ voice, pealing out into the unclean silence of the chapel's gloom, beating against the curved and shining walls which sent back clashing paeans of tremendous harmony—

"Thus I have conquered, ye Genii of the Twelve hours!

Thus are all things subdued to my Will!

By wisdom I have pierced Truth.

By intelligence I have cast down idols.

By strength I have bound Death in chains.

By patience I have fathomed the Infinite.

THE SIN EATER

Now is the Universe wholly revealed to me.
Ye Terrible Ones! Princes of the kingdoms and
heavens of Pharzuph, of Sialul, of Aeglun,
of Aclahayr,
I, who have worshipped and obeyed, shall serve
no more.
Princes c' Earth, of Air, of Fire, of Water,
The Four Elements you rule are as dust under my
heel.
I am invulnerable—beyond Death and change
forever.
The six wings of Bereschott cover me.
The Rock of Yesod beneath my feet.
Bow down in homage! BOW DOWN!"

Sant, his eyes on the tense convulsed
figure, saw it sway. Its outflung arms
dropped.
The dark head leaned back—back until
Sant could see its greenish pallor, and half-
veiled eyes. Rigid, entranced, the spirit
within him caught up into dark swooning
ecstasy, Stephen fell back slowly, slowly
into Sant's waiting arms.

"FRIDAY afternoon! A few more hours,
Adrian—only a few hours now."
Sant glanced at Rosaina, got up from his
chair and began to walk up and down his
study. Presently he lighted a pipe, let it go
out between his clenched teeth as he paced
to and fro. He looked out across his garden
where violets, anemones and jonquils braved
February winds and tall daffodils danced to
its piping. His absent gaze followed the
course of a valley and rested at last on the
stretch of ocean beyond. Gray, turbulent as

his own thoughts, the Atlantic lay under a
leaden sky. His brooding look dwelt on it
as if in this vast element he found ease for
his soul.
"Adrian!"
He turned back to Rosaina, sitting by
the fire, his heart contracted with pity at
sight of her. How altered since Zennor's
death! Not all the tragic years of her marriage had broken her as these few days of
torturing anxiety for the man she loved.
Sant's burden grew heavier as he met
her eyes; she looked so lost, so wild, so
grief-stricken; her body seemed transparent
in the firelit dusk; her golden hair was
lifeless and faded, the delicate lines of
face and neck painfully evident, the amber
eyes two deep pools of weariness. Body,
mind and spirit could endure little more.
And yet they *must!* And tonight. There
could be no halt in the tremendous impetus
of the occult rhythm of events. Zennor,
through his chosen medium, Stephen Lynn,
could not himself alter the impending climax now. Tonight he gained all, or lost
all. There was no middle course.
He had challenged the Four Ancient
Ones, and must prove their master or be
forever enslaved. Tonight he must achieve
the goal for which he had striven since his
first incarnation on earth by offering the
Perfect Sacrifice to complete the Triad of his
protection.
Tonight! That much Zennor had revealed
through Stephen on the day of the funeral
while Sant watched in the chapel. And because it was tonight, Sant knew his enemy

23

feared him and his influence; for Zennor's own baneful star would not be at its zenith until the next moon's waning, in the Tenth Hour, called Malaen.

The genii of that Hour were strong and slaves to Zennor's will. They had been the heat of his blood, the shadow of his body, the breath of his nostrils when—in his first life on earth—he had, in shaggy beast-like form, run on all fours through forests of the north, forests dug up now as coal from under the crust of the world. Tonight these genii would serve him well. The Hour was favorable—but less favorable than the Tenth Hour, called Malaen. Zennor would have been stronger in the next moon's waning.

He went back to Rosaina, drew up a chair beside her. No hint of anxiety showed in the tranquil face he turned to her. He did not doubt her courage now, but he doubted whether the frail hold she had on life would carry her through the ordeal required of it. And she must live. *She must defeat Zennor on this plane while in the flesh.* Divorced from her body, he could not help her. Her ego and Stephen's too would be incorporated with Zennor's, made one with his damned soul.

She voiced his thoughts.

"I shouldn't have lasted another twenty-four hours. Another night. The night, oh God! Adrian!"

He bit hard on his pipe-stem and nodded.

"Even though you sat outside my door to keep watch, to prevent his coming to me, he sent his devils to torment me. Your drugs gave sleep to my body but my spirit suffered. In the shadows—in the silence I could see my body lying there, while I—myself—was forced to listen to what They said—what They said!"

"The main thing was that you slept. Your reason was saved in spite of all he could do."

He had never let her see how perilous he knew those dreams of hers to be. He only marveled at the strong beautiful balance of her mind that retained its sanity in spite of them.

A BUMP at the door heralded the sturdy old housekeeper with a tea-tray. She was the only servant Sant had permitted to stay on since the ceremony he had witnessed in the chapel. He refused to expose two younger maids to the danger of Stephen's presence in the house, or, rather, to the satanic malice of the mind now in possession of Stephen's body.

"I'll go myself to let Mr. Lynn know that tea is ready," he told the old servant.

Mrs. Poldhu nodded. She was a rather formidable old woman, afraid of no one and given to expressing her opinions very forcibly indeed. She'd summed up Stephen as "the spit of that old toad, his uncle Mark Zennor" and had flatly refused to speak or look at him.

"Plaze yourself, sir. Tesn't no consarn o' mine."

Sant left Rosaina setting out the tea-things. Hároon Er-Rasheed lay before the fire, bestowing passionate attention on one large paw which failed to meet his standards of cleanliness. Mrs. Poldhu waddled off to get more coal for the dying fire.

Sant searched the garden in vain. Satisfied that Stephen was no longer there, he hurried indoors again. He hadn't been in the least concerned about the tea question but had seen, from the window, that Stephen was warily approaching a gate on which a blackbird sang in the dusk. Sant didn't wish a repetition of a savage little incident he and Rosaina had witnessed yesterday when Stephen had revoltingly injured a dog that had snarled at him.

That was his voice! Sant hurried. The door of the study, where he'd left Rosaina, was open.

"Stand still, little fool!"

The words rang out.

"This is to punish you for locking me out at night. Now, you yellow beast—*jump!*"

Sant leaped to the door and was in time to see Hároon Er-Rasheed between Stephen's hands, his belly flattened to the ground, ears back, golden eyes black with terror. At the word "jump!" the animal shot forward as if from a gun.

Rosaina stood, white, agonized unable to stir a muscle. Her shriek and Stephen's laugh synchronized with Sant's lightning dash. He caught up the yellow cat from the fire on which it crouched, its eyes glazed and fixed on Stephen's face.

The animal stubbornly reisisted Sant. It

fought to free itself, struggled furiously to obey the will of the mocking devil in Stephen's eyes. Sant held it in iron hands, and faced its tormentor.

"Mark Zennor!" his voice was barely a whisper. "You exceed your powers. Release this animal—I lay my command on you!"

In Stephen's eyes such cold blind hatred flared that Rosaina cried out again. But Sant moved nearer to his enemy, stared him between the eyes—stared until the dark fire in them was quenched, until their lids drooped. In sullen obedience his hand brushed the big cat's head. He muttered a low-breathed word.

The Persian jumped half the width of the room, halted to turn eyes of blazing yellow fire on Stephen, dashed like a crazy thing through an open window, flashed across a lawn, up over a wall, and away. Stephen also vanished from Rosaina's sight.

He went slowly, but his exit was even more spectacular than that of the unfortunate beast. Again she cried out in stark terror, for he disappeared without moving at all.

"He is here with us, Rosaina. He is perfectly visible to me. But you are, in part, subject to him. He has intoxicated your vision by a trick. *Will* yourself to see him—here, take my hand."

A touch of it, and she regained control. She saw Stephen walking toward the door.

SANT looked after him as he went from the room.

"He lost control too. I've tried for that revelation from the start. Oh, it was an infinitesimal moment of anger merely, but enough—enough to work on. He's at a disadvantage in his borrowed flesh."

Rosaina trembled, but with anger now, rather than fear.

"Adrian! Your poor cat—won't you go and look for him?"

Her indignation burned so fiercely that she couldn't fathom his apparent indifference. He gave her a long keen look.

"You are very angry. Good! It will stimulate you. But don't worry about Hároon. Mercifully he wasn't injured; the fire was almost out and his fur's thick. He'll forget when—when we've saved Stephen."

She was goaded to new activity. The shock of the beautiful friendly beast's punishment, remembrance of his glazed eyes fixed on Stephen's grinning face, and his shining yellow fur with gray smoke curling up about his body, stung her to fierce anger and revolt.

"You're right. He shall not take Stephen from me—he shall not! I'll fight, I'll fight to the end now. That poor cat's eyes—Stephen shall never . . . oh! I'm ready, Adrian! That devil shall not win!"

He knew her present condition could not last, but it all helped. Anger would die down, her mood of hot reckless indignation cool. Only staying-power counted. But this would strengthen her will. Everything turned finally on that.

"There's work for both of us to do before midnight. And I want to emphasize once more that it's very important you should go of your own free will tonight. I must remain here, working for you, helping to strengthen your will with my own. But it is Zennor's chosen Hour and I may not interfere with what he does. Don't evade Stephen. Offer yourself a free victim for the sacrifice. And concentrate ceaselessly, on your purpose to save Stephen."

"Yes! Yes!" she whispered, "I must hold him! Save him!"

"Hold him, save him," emphasized her companion. "And now there's no time to

transported to a world Rosaina couldn't conceive of.

She recollected the yellow Persian's queer interest in these literary labors, how he'd leaped up at the faint rustle of twig on paper when a new symbol had been drawn, how his eyes, their pupils distended to the edge of the iris, had followed the movements of some invisible moving thing about Sant's chair.

Poor beautiful Hároon! She bent to her task with tightened lips.

BY SLOW degrees she became aware of her surroundings. When first Stephen led her to a throne-like seat, she could make out nothing in the pungent dusk. Now the great chapel was revealing itself; and, instructed by Adrian though she was, her heart stood still at the revelation.

Her throne was in the exact center of the great circular floor. Behind it, and on either side, curved the shining walls.

Before her stood the altar with its reredos which, from this distance, she saw only as a burning patch of light.

She scarcely glanced at the great dazzling globe of metal in midair, so afraid was she of its will-benumbing magic. She fixed her gaze, rather, on the man who moved to and fro before the altar in its refracted rays—going about his awful business.

Her chill, slender hands clasped the snakes' heads of polished ebony that formed two arms for her seat. The elaborate ritual that was to culminate in her death was begun. She recalled Adrian, shut up in his study, bent over his desk, concentrating on her, sending out his strong will to aid her own. Strengthened, steadied, she then deliberately thrust aside this mental image and gave her whole attention to Stephen and his profane and terrifying preparations.

Mark's sin-eater—Mark himself now, save for the thin veil of flesh that masked his hell-born vicious soul. It was Stephen's straight strong body there, kneeling at the altar. It was his dear hands, his dark head, his face and eyes and lips. Oh! it was everything—and it was nothing. The mad cruel smile, the eyes' wild glare, the towering merciless pride that blazed behind this fleshly screen were Mark's alone.

Mark's sin-eater. And how deep was

lose. You've got those books and papers? Good. Concentrate for your life—and his. No need to lock ourselves in tonight. Stephen will be at Lamorna House—until he comes for you."

He was at once absorbed, drawing strange symbols on ancient brittle papyri where faint tracery of lettering showed. After examining these faint marks through a glass for minutes at a time, he repeated them aloud. At the last word—all he said being perfectly unintelligible to the girl—he would scratch a new sign on the papyrus under his hand with an alder twig which he kept charred at a naked flame on his desk.

He'd been at this for two days and two nights, slaving like a man possessed, muttering, writing, glaring at the dirty old papyri, every sin of the dead printed upon this face and body of Stephen Lynn! The voice that rang in deep imperious rhythm was altogether Mark's. Stephen's had been notably clear, eager, flexible, with a trick of rising inflection that she adored.

Ah! This was Mark! That he moved and spoke in Stephen's guise made him more awfully Mark Zennor. Not a glimpse of the real Stephen. Not a spark of his own ego burned in the temple of his body; its altar light was quenched and Mark's dark soul was in possession.

Rosaina's courage wavered. Suppose Adrian was wrong? Suppose Stephen could not, after all, return to his habitation of the flesh for the promised moment? Suppose she failed to recognize the moment if it came? What had Adrian said?

"Stephen will come. He *must* come. Zennor may not offer sacrifice without first allowing Stephen to return momentarily to his own body once more. Beyond all question you will see him again in the flesh.."

Fear drove hope away, rode her leaping thoughts.

"He is not here—the man I love is not here. This is a devil, a monster, it is Mark. He has tricked Stephen, destroyed him, thrust him down to hell—his eyes—Stephen's kind gentle eyes—that cat, how his eyes were held by Mark's! . . . Stephen too, he must obey, torture himself, he is a slave—a slave like that animal! Stephen! But there *is* no Stephen—he has no body, no soul, he doesn't exist! Stephen!"

But love still struggled to believe.

"I must wait. One moment there will be, one brief moment! I shall meet him face to face in the living flesh. My dear! My beloved! And I will hold him fast—fast for ever. No one shall take him from me. He will come and I will hold him fast—fast—"

And now the chapel lights grew dim. The suspended dazzling globe of metal dulled to a pale moonglow. Black candles, tall watchful guardians about the altar-stone, bowed trembling heads of flame, bowed down to their sockets, wavered—died. Only the reredos still blazed, its restless secret fire more brilliant, more incandescent as globe and candles failed.

Stephen turned from the altar, advanced with stately purposeful deliberation, down

the five steps, across the chapel floor. Now he stood before Rosaina and in his brilliant eyes she saw Mark's demon enthroned, triumphant.

"Come!" he commanded. "I am ready. You are chosen to share this Hour with me."

She felt his fingers close upon her own; their heat burned her, their cruel strength appalled. This was Mark, all Mark indeed. How well she knew that fierce hold, how her nerves shrank at its familiar possessiveness!

He led her to a thin, blood-red crescent of moon that gleamed in its first quarter on the marble floor. Vast eagles' wings outstretched in fiery lines behind the wicked knife-edge of the moon.

"Stand here."

Obediently she placed her feet upon the sign. She felt its poignant blade's sharp agony. The High Priest, hands of iron on her shoulders, faced her with rapt cruel face down-bent.

"Receive her, oh Prince and Ruler of the Air! This is the victim appointed to fulfil my Destiny. Before Time began I chose her from all the worlds that are. Her blood shall seal my vow."

She felt the beat of great wings; the air about her vibrated and fanned her coldly on the cheek, cold as the breath from mountain heights, cold to the heart it struck—but the High Priest's face of triumph chilled her very soul.

He led her to the east, where a half-moon showed—a fountain of living water rising beside it. Here again he dedicated her, calling on all the waters of the earth to witness his power.

By the three-quarter moon dark earth was strewn, and, standing here, she knew the smothering darkness of the grave. Only the unrelenting hand that guided her, the deep voice that pealed in trumpet-call, summoned her again from what seemed her tomb.

And now he set her feet upon the last ominous moon in whose full orb moved that potent deadly cloud—soul of all that is —ageless—indestructible—accursed.

A brazier of fire stood close by. The High Priest drew a tiny phial from the folds of his robe, shook its powdered contents on the red coals. Flame leaped in a twisting clear blue pillar to the roof, spread across it, streamed down the walls again.

The High Priest's voice rolled in thrilling music above the elements' fierce roar:

"Rulers of Fire—above the earth, within the earth, about the earth!
Michael! Samuel! Anael! Hear me now!
The appointed Hour is come! The Victim is prepared
Receive my Sacrifice! Receive my Sacrifice! Receive my Sacrifice!"

As the third loud cry rang echoing round the chapel's flaming walls, one single spear of glittering white fire thrust upward from the cradle of its being—from the deadly ovoid cloud within the full red moon. The priest's hand closed swiftly about the fire-spear, bent it to brush Rosaina's forehead, released it with a muttered word. Instantly the spear vanished and all the fiery walls and roof grew dark once more.

Down to his knees sank the High Priest. His lips touched the red moon's rim. Three times he did obeisance, three times he murmured words of power. Then he rose and faced the victim.

Rosaina, at touch of the shining spear, felt deadly mortal chill invade her body—a sense of doom paralyzed every faculty.

It was too late to struggle, too late to fight! Stephen was lost! And she must die! She must let go—let go—let go. . . .

She stood watching the High Priest as he moved from her, up the five steps, up to the altar. He reached it, turned to face her, lifted his arms until his black silken cloak stretched like wings on either side of a scarlet sheath-like robe. Higher leaped the hellish lights behind the reredos. Before its strong pulsating evil, Stephen loomed dark and tall and terrible. He waited for her. He summoned her. She must obey—obey him.

From the caves of darkness that lined the walls between its broad squat pillars, shadows thrust and crowded, worshippers from hell, incorporeal, soundless, shapeless, fluid as water, bodiless as smoke, yet, beyond all words, instinct with power.

The High Priest's congregation was assembled. Rosaina the Victim was summoned. Cold and darkness below, above, on every side. She moved to the altar like driftwood borne on the ocean tide.

Now she was at the altar steps. Each one's ascent set her a world's width farther off from Stephen. Now she stood in the balefire glow of the altar-screen. The High Priest's hands lifted her, laid her on the altar-stone.

At last she saw the figures on the gleaming quivering reredos, saw herself in the bound victim there, saw Stephen in the High Priest who stood beside the sacrificial stone. And behind the veils of the Four about the altar, she recognized the lewd companions of her dream.

A swift pang of longing tore her for Adrian's help. How sure he had been! How utterly she had believed that Stephen—Stephen himself—would return if only for an instant. Now, turning to the wickedly intent face bent over her she saw Mark, and Mark alone.

Stephen was lost—forever lost. And she must die and go out in the darkness too.

Thin biting cords were bound about her. A knife-blade winked and flashed. Now indeed the end was come. Her eyes stared up into the face bent over hers.

Sudden rending pain stung her failing senses. A veil seemed snatched from before her eyes. Her heart's slow beat quickened to furious pulsing life. Nerve and muscle strained to break the bonds that held her.

"Stephen! Stephen! Stephen!"

Her voice rang through the gloom. The black smooth walls seemed to quiver in response. All the hurtling swarming shadows jostled closer.

"Stephen! Stephen!"

Again the dark walls trembled. Closer pressed the demon shadows.

"Stephen! Come to me! Come to me!"

The High Priest's face bent lower. Dark eyes looked into her own. A faint urgent whisper reached her ears.

"I have come . . . from hell . . . to you. Hold me! Save me!"

"Stephen!" she cried again. "Ah, this is you indeed! Your eyes that look at me, Stephen! I will hold you. I will save you. Keep your eyes on mine. I will never, never let you go!"

And now she died a thousand deaths. Delusion hurled her from world to world through awful space. Fire burned her flesh from her charred bones. Water drowned her beneath dark mountainous waves. Heavy earth buried her in earthquake shocks. But in flame and rushing water, under the earth or above it in the illimitable aching kingdoms of the air, she saw one thing clearly. She saw the face of Stephen Lynn. Nothing —nothing else.

Fighting, struggling, holding the gates of her will fast locked against Mark's vicious power, she felt a hand in hers. It was Adrian's strong clasp. Adrian's voice spoke across the roar of fire and tumult of water, of crashing rocks and howling winds.

"The Hour is about to strike. Hold fast, hold fast!"

Stephen's face grew clearer. Its look altered. He was smiling down at her. She could feel his warm breath. His strong gentle hands released her from her bonds. His voice spoke, assuring her of safety. His arms enfolded her as she sank, faint with rapture . . . the world about her fading. . . .

"BUT Adrian! You did come to me!" she protested. "I saw you, heard you, felt your hand in mine."

"Probably. All of me that really *is* me. But my body didn't move from this room, this table, this chair you see before you."

Rosaina looked round the room. Sun streamed in from open windows. A blackbird's exquisite liquid song opened the very gates of heaven to its listeners. She turned to Stephen once more.

He put out a hand to touch her own.

"Yes! Still here, darling."

"I can't—I can't believe it. The three of us together at last—safe—happy—free!"

"And Mark—" she shuddered. "Tell me, Adrian, I want to know before we forget him—utterly. What happened—what does our freedom mean—to *him?*"

Sant put out a quick warning hand. His answer came muffled, almost a whisper:

"Forget, forget, Rosaina! His dark soul is in bondage. It is not safe, even in thought, to follow him now."

Stephen's arm drew her to him. His eyes adored her.

"Rose, golden Rose! Remember only that we are happy—free—at last."

Living Buddhess

By SEABURY QUINN

A fascinating tale of a living female Buddha and the dreadful change that befell a lovely American girl—a tale of Jules de Grandin, and a dire lama from devil-ridden Asia

THE hot, erotic rhythm of the rumba beat upon our ears with the repercussive vibrance of a voodoo drum. White dinner coated men guided partners clad in sheerest of sheer crêpes or air-light muslin in the mazes of the negroid dance across the umber tiles which floored the Graystone Towers Roof. Waiters hastened silent-footed with their trays of tall, iced drinks. The purple, star-gemmed sky seemed near enough to touch.

"Tired, old chap?" I asked de Grandin as he patted back a yawn and gazed disconsolately at his glass of dubonnet. "Shall we be going?"

"*Tiens*, we might as well," he answered with a slightly weary smile; "there is small pleasure in watching others—*grand cochon vert*, and what is that?"

"What's what?" I asked, noting with surprize how his air of boredom dropped away and little wrinkles of intensive thought etched suddenly about the corners of his eyes.

"The illumination yonder," he nodded toward the bunting-wrapped stanchions on the parapet between which swung the gently-swaying festoons of electric lights, "surely that is not provided by the management. It looks like *feu Saint-Elme*."

Following his glance I noticed that a globe of luminosity flickered from the tallest of the light-poles, wavering to and fro like a yellow candle-flame blown by the wind; but there was no wind; the night was absolutely stirless.

"H'm, it does look like St. Elmo's fire, at that," I acquiesced, "but how——"

"*Ps-s-s-t!*" he shut me off. "Observe him, if you please!"

Bobbing aimlessly, like a wasp that bounces on the ceiling of the room to which it has made inadvertent entrance, the pear-shaped globe of luminance had detached itself from the gilt ball at the top of the light standard, and was weaving an erratic pattern back and forth above the dancers. Almost at the center of the floor it paused uncertainly, as if it had been a balloon caught between two rival drafts, then suddenly dropped down, landing on the high-coiled copper-colored hair of a young woman.

It fluttered weavingly above the clustered curls of her coiffure a moment like a pentecostal flame, then with a sudden dip descended on the cupric hair, spread about it like a halo for an instant, and vanished; not like a bursting bubble, but slowly, like a ponderable substance being sucked in, as milk in a tall goblet vanishes when imbibed through a straw.

I do not think that anybody else observed the strange occurrence, for the dancers were too hypnotized by sensuous motion and the moaning rhythm of the music, while the diners were preoccupied with food; but the scream the girl emitted as the flickering flame sank through her high-dressed hair brought everyone up standing. It was, I thought, not so much a cry of pain as of insanity, of strange disease and maniacal excitement. It frothed and spouted from her tortured mouth like a geyser of unutterable anguish.

"Mordieu, see to her, my friend, she swoons!" de Grandin cried as we dashed across the dance floor where the girl lay in a heap, like a lovely tailor's dummy overturned and broken.

With the assistance of two waiters, chaperoned by an assistant manager in near-hysterics, we took her to the ladies' rest room and laid her on a couch. She was breathing stertorously, her hands were clenched, and as I reached to feel her pulse I noticed that her skin was cold and clammy as a frog's, and little hum-

mocks of horripilation showed upon her forearms. "Every symptom of lightning-stroke," I murmured as I felt her feeble, fluttering pulse and turned her lids back to find pupils so dilated that they all but hid her irides; "is there any sign of burns?"

"One moment, we will see," de Grandin answered, stripping off her flaring-skirted frock of white organza and the clinging slip of primavera printed satin as one might turn a glove. We had no difficulty in examination, for except for a lace bandeau bound about her bosom and a pair of absolutely minimal gilt-leather

"Atop the perfect, cream-white body was another face, an old face, a wicked face, a face with Mongoloid features."

sandals she was, as Jules de Grandin might have said, "as naked as his hand." Her skin was white and fine and smooth, with that appearance of translucence seen so often in red-headed people, and nowhere did it show a trace of burn or blemish. But even as we finished our inspection a choking, rasping wheeze came in her throat, and her stiffened body fell back lax and flaccid.

"Quickly," cried de Grandin as he turned her on her face, knelt above her and began administering artificial respiration; "have warm blankets and some brandy brought, my friend. I will keep her heart and lungs in action till the stimulants arrive."

ALMOST an hour had elapsed when the girl's lids finally fluttered up, disclosing sea-green eyes that held a dreamy, slightly melancholy look. "Where am—I?" she asked feebly, voicing the almost universal question of the fainting. "Why —you're men, aren't you?"

"We are so taken and considered, Mademoiselle," de Grandin answered with a smile. "You had expected otherwise?"

"I—don't—know," she answered listlessly; then, as she saw her badly frightened escort at the door: "Oh, George, I think I must have died for a few moments!"

De Grandin motioned the young man to a chair beside the couch, tucked a blanket-end more snugly round the girl's slim shoulders, and bent a smile of almost fatherly affection on the lovers. "Corbleu, Mademoiselle, we—Doctor Trowbridge and I—feared you were going to die permanently," he assured her. "You were a very ill young woman."

"But what was it?" asked the young man. "One moment Sylvia and I were dancing peacefully, the next she screamed and fainted, and——"

"Précisément, Monsieur, one is permit-

ted to indulge in speculation as to what it was," de Grandin nodded. "One wonders greatly. To all appearances le feu Saint Elme—the how do you call him? Saint Elmo's light?—took form upon a flagstaff by the dancing-roof, but that should happen only during periods of storm when the air is charged with electricity. No matter, it appeared to form and dance about the pole-tops like a naughty little child who torments a wandering blind man, then pouf! the globe of fire, he did detach himself and fall like twenty thousand bricks on Mademoiselle. This should not be. Saint Elmo's light is usually harmless as the gleaming of the firefly in the dark. Like good old wine, it is beautiful but mild. Yet there it is; it struck your lady's head and struck her all unconscious at the selfsame time.

"What was your sensation, Mademoiselle?" he added, turning from the young man to the girl.

"I hardly know," she answered in a voice so weak it seemed to be an echo. "I had no warning. I was dancing with George and thinking how nice it would be when the rumba finished and we could go back and get a drink, when suddenly something seemed to fall on me—no, that's not quite right, I didn't feel as if a falling object struck me, but rather as if I had received a heavy, stunning blow from a club or some such weapon, and as though every hair in my head was being pulled out by the roots at the same time. Then something seemed to spread and grow inside my head, pushing out against my skull and flesh and skin until the pain became so great I couldn't stand it. Then my whole head seemed to burst apart, like an exploding bomb, and——"

"And there you were," the young man interrupted with a nervous laugh.

She gave him a long, troubled look from heavily-fringed eyes. "There I was," she assented. "But where?"

"Why, knocked all in a heap, my dear. We thought you were a goner. You would have been, too, if these two gentlemen hadn't happened to be doctors, and dining at the table next to us."

"That isn't what I mean," she answered with a little, puzzled frown. "I was—I *went* somewhere while I was unconscious, dear. I—I half believe I died and had a glimpse of Paradise—only it wasn't at all as I'd imagined it."

"Oh, nonsense, Syl," her sweetheart chided. "Maybe you imagined you saw something while you were out cold, but——"

"Tell us what it was you saw, *Mademoiselle*," de Grandin interrupted in a soothing voice. "How did your vision differ from your preconceived idea of Paradise?"

She lay in quiet thought a moment, her green eyes wide and dreamy, almost wistful. Finally: "I seemed to be in a great Oriental city. The buildings were of stone and towered like the Empire State and Chrysler buildings. Their tops were overlaid with gold leaf or sheet copper that shone so brilliantly that it fairly burned my eyes as the fierce sun beat down from a cloudless sky. I was on a portico or terrace of some sort, looking down a wide street reaching to a thick, high-gated wall, and through this gate came a procession. Hundreds of men on horseback carried lances from which silk flags fluttered, and after them came musicians with drums and flutes and tambourines and cymbals, and the music that they made was lovely. Then there were marching women, walking with a kind of dancing step and singing as they came. There were jewels and flowers in their straight, black hair, jewels in their ears and noses, necklaces of beaten gold and pearls and rubies and carved coral around their throats, and jeweled bands of gold around their arms and wrists. Bright gems flashed in the chain-gold belts that clasped their waists; around their ankles they had wire circlets hung with bells that chimed like laughter as they walked. They wore skirts of bright vermilion tied with girdles of blue silk, and their hands and toes and lips and nipples were all dyed brilliant red. Next came a great array of soldiers bearing shields and lances, then more musicians, and finally a herd of elephants which, like the women, wore belled bands of gold around their ankles. But while the women's bells were sweet and clear and high, the gongs upon the elephants were deep and soft and mellow, like the deep notes of marimbas, and the bass and treble bell-notes blended in a harmony that set the pulses going like the beat of syncopated music."

"*Eh bien, Mademoiselle*, this Paradise you saw was colorful, however much it may have lacked in orthodoxy," de Grandin smiled. But there was no answering gleam of humor in the girl's green eyes as she looked at him almost beseechingly.

"It thrilled me and elated me," she said. "I seemed to understand it all, and to know that this procession was for *me*, and me alone; but it frightened me, as well."

"You were afraid? But why?"

"Because, although I knew what it was all about, I didn't."

De Grandin cast a look of humorous entreaty at the young man seated by the couch. "Will you translate for me, *Monsieur?* Me, I have resided in your so splendid country but a scant twelve years, and I fear I do not understand the English fluently. I thought I heard her say she understood, yet failed to understand. But no, it cannot be. My ears or wits play the *mauvaise farce* with me."

"I don't quite know how to express it," the girl responded. "I seemed to be two people, myself and another. It was that other one who understood the pageant and who gloried in it, and that's what frightened me, for that other one who knew that the procession was to honor him was a man, while I was still a woman, and——" She paused, and tears formed in her eyes, but whether she were weeping for lost womanhood or from vexation at her inability to find the words to frame her explanation I could not decide.

"Come, come, young lady; that's enough," I ordered in my sternest bedside manner. "You've suffered from a heavy shock, and people in such cases often have queer visions. There's nothing medically curious in your having seen this circus parade while you were unconscious, and that feeling of dual personality is quite in keeping, too. If you feel strong enough, I suggest you get your clothes on and let us take you home."

"Q UEER what aberrations people have following electric shock," I mused as we paused in the pantry for a final good-night drink. "I remember when I was an interne at City Hospital I had an ambulance case where a woman had been struck by a live wire fallen from a trolley pole. All the way back to the hospital she insisted that she was a cow, and lowed continuously. Now, take this Dearborn girl——"

"Precisely, take her, if you please," de Grandin nodded, his mouth half full of cheese and biscuit, a foaming mug of beer raised half-way to his lips. "Is hers not a case to marvel at? She is struck down all but dead by a ball of harmless *feu Saint-Elme,* and while unconscious sees the vision of a thing entirely outside her experience or background. She could not have dreamed it, for we dream only that of which we know at least a little, yet——" He drained his mug of beer,

dusted off his fingers and raised his shoulders in a shrug. *"Tenez,"* he yawned, "let the devil worry with it. Me, I have the craving for ten hours' sleep."

I T WAS shortly after dinner the next evening that my office telephone began a clangor which refused to be denied. When, worn down at last by the persistence of the caller, I barked a curt "Hullo?" into the instrument, a woman's voice came tremblingly. "Doctor Trowbridge, this is Mrs. Henry Dearborn of 1216 Passaic Boulevard. You and Doctor de Grandin attended my daughter Sylvia when she fainted at Graystone Towers last night?"

"Yes," I admitted.

"May I ask you to come over? Doctor Rusholt, our family physician, is out of town, and since you're already familiar with Sylvia's case——"

"What seems to be the trouble?" I cut in. "Any evidence of burning? Sometimes that develops later in such cases, and——"

"No, thank heaven, physically she seems all right, but a little while ago she complained of feeling nervous, and declared she couldn't be comfortable in any position. She took some aromatic spirits of ammonia and lay down, thinking it would pass away, but found herself too much wrought up to rest. Then she started walking up and down, and suddenly she began muttering to herself, clasping and unclasping her hands and twitching her face like a person with Saint Vitus' dance. A few minutes ago she fainted, and seems to be in some sort of delirium, for she's still muttering and twitching her hands and feet——"

"All right," I cut the flow of symptoms short; "we'll be right over.

"Looks as if the Dearborn girl's developing chorea following her shock last night," I told de Grandin as we headed for the patient's house. "Poor child, I'm afraid she's in for a bad time."

"Agreed," he nodded solemnly. "I fear that he has managed to break in——."

"Whatever are you maundering about? —at your confounded ghost-hunting again?" I interrupted testily.

"Not at all, by no means; quite the contrary," he assured me. "This time, my friend, I damn think that the ghost has hunted us. He has, to use your quaint American expression, absconded with our garments while we bathed."

SYLVIA DEARBORN lay upon the high-dressed bed, her burnished-copper hair and milky skin a charming contrast to her apple-green percale pajamas. She was not conscious, but certainly she was not sleeping, for at times her eyes would open violently, as though they had been actuated by an unoiled mechanism, and her arms and legs would twitch with sharp, erratic gestures. Sometimes she moaned as though in frightful torment; again her lips would writhe and twist as though they had volition of their own, and once or twice she seemed about to speak, but only senseless jabber issued from her drooling mouth.

De Grandin leant across the bed, listening intently to the gibberish she babbled, finally straightened with a shrug and turned to me. "*La morphine?*" he suggested.

"I should think so," I replied, preparing a half-grain injection. "We must control these spasms or she'll wear herself out."

Deftly he swabbed her arm with alcohol, took a fold of skin between his thumb and forefinger and held it ready for the needle. I shot the mercy-bearing liquid home, and stood to wait results. Gradually her grotesque movements

quieted, her moans became more feeble, and in a little while she slept.

"Give her this three times a day, and see that she remains in bed," I ordered, writing a prescription for Fowler's solution. "I don't think you'll need us, but if any change occurs please don't hesitate to call."

MRS. DEARBORN took me at my word. The blue, fading twilight of early dawn limned the windows of my chamber when the bedside telephone began its heartless, sleep-destroying stutter, and I groaned with something close akin to anguish as I reached for it.

"Oh, Doctor Trowbridge, won't you come at once?" the mother's frightened voice implored. "Sylvia's had another seizure, worse—much worse—this time. She's talking almost constantly, but it seems she's speaking in a foreign language, and somehow she seems *changed!*"

Years of practise had made me adept at quick dressing, but de Grandin bettered my best efforts. He was waiting for me in the hall, debonair and well-groomed with his usual spruce immaculateness, and had even found time to select a flower for his buttonhole from the epergne in the dining-room.

A single glance sufficed to tell us that our patient suffered something more than simple chorea. The pseudo-purposive gesticulations were no longer evident; indeed, she seemed as rigid as she had been the night before when we treated her for lightning-shock, and her skin was corpse-cold to the touch. But her lips were working constantly, and a steady flow of words ran from them. At first I thought it only senseless gabble, but a moment's listening told me that the sounds were words, though of what language I could not determine. They were sing-songed, now high, now low, with irregularly stressed accents, and, somehow, reminded me of the jargon Chinese laundrymen are wont to use when talking to each other. Queerly, too, at times her voice assumed a different timbre, almost high falsetto, but definitely masculine. Constantly recurring through her mumbled gabble was the phrase: *"Oom mani padme—oom mani padme! Hong!"*

"Do something for her, Doctor! Oh, for the love of heaven, help her!" Mrs. Dearborn begged as she ushered us into her daughter's bedroom; then, as I laid my kit upon a chair: "Look—look at her face!"

Whatever changes may be present in his patients'—or his patients' relatives' —appearance, a doctor has to keep a poker face, but retaining even outward semblance of unruffled nerves was hard as I looked in Sylvia Dearborn's countenance. A weird, uncanny metamorphosis seemed taking place. As though her features had been formed of plastic substance, and that substance was being worked by the unseen hands of some invisible modeler, her very cast of countenance was in process of transshaping. Somehow, the lips seemed thickened, bulbous, and drooped at the corners like those of one whose facial muscles had been weakened by prolonged indulgence in the practise of all seven deadly sins, and as the mouth sagged, so the outer corners of the eyes appeared to lift, the cast of features was definitely Mongol; the slant-eyed, thick-lipped face of a Mongolian idiot was replacing Sylvia Dearborn's cameo-clear countenance.

"Oom mani padme—oom mani padme!" moaned the girl upon the bed, and at each repetition her voice rose till the chant became a wail and the wail became a scream; dry-throated, rasping, horrible in its intensity: *"Oom mani padme—oom mani padme! Hong!"*

"Whatever——" I began, but de Grandin leaped across the room, staring

as in fascination at the sick girl's changing features, then turned to me with a low command:

"Morphine; much more morphine, good Friend Trowbridge, if you please! Make the dose so strong that one more millionth of a grain would cause her death; but give it quickly. We must throw her speaking-apparatus out of gear, make it utterly impossible for her to go through the mechanics of repeating that vile invocation!"

I hastened to comply, and as Sylvia sank into inertia from the drug:

"Come, my friend, come away," he bade. "We must go at once and get advice from one who knows whereof he speaks. She will be all right for a short time; the drug will not wear off for several hours."

"Where the dickens are we going?" I demanded as he urged me to make haste.

"To New York, my friend, to that potpourri of intermixed humanity that they call Chinatown. Oh, make speed, my friend! We must hasten, we must rush; we must travel with the speed of light if we would be in time, believe me!"

W HERE Doyers Street makes a snake-back turn on its way toward the Bowery stood the taciturn-faced red-brick house, flanked on one side by a curio-dealer's ménage whose windows showed a bewildering miscellany of Chinese curiosa designed for sale at swollen prices to the tourist trade and on the other by a dingy eating-house grandiloquently mislabeled The Palace of Seven Thousand Gustatory Felicities. Shuttered windows like sleeping eyes faced toward the narrow, winding street; the door was flush with the front wall and seemed at first glance to be rather inexpertly grained wood. A second look showed it was painted metal, and from the sharp, unvibrant sound the knocker gave as de

Grandin jerked it up and down, I knew the metal was as thick and solid as the steel wall of a safe..

Three times the little Frenchman plied the knocker, beating a sharp, broken rhythm, and as he let the ring fall with a final thump there came an almost soundless *click* and a hidden panel in the door slipped back, disclosing a small peep-hole. Behind the spy-hole was an eye, small, sharp and piercing as a bird's, curious as a monkey's, which inspected us from head to foot. Then came a guttural *"Kungskee-kungskee,"* and the metal door swung open to admit us to a hall where a lantern of pierced brass cast a subdued orange glow on apricot-hung walls, floors strewn with thick-piled Chinese rugs, carved black-wood chairs and tables, last of all a crystal image of the Buddha enthroned upon a pedestal of onyx.

Our usher was a small man dressed in the black-silk jacket and loose trousers once common to Celestials everywhere, but now as out of date with them as Gladstone collars and bell-shaped beaver hats are in New York. Tucking hands demurely in his jacket sleeves, he made three quick bows to de Grandin, murmuring the courteous *"Kungskee-kungskee"* at each bow. The little Frenchman responded in the same way, and, the ceremony finished, asked slowly, "Your honorable master, is he to be seen? We have traveled far and fast, and seek his counsel in a pressing matter."

The Oriental bowed again and motioned toward a chair. "Deign to take honorable seating while this inconsequential person sees if the Most Worshipful may be approached," he answered in a flat and level voice. There was hardly any trace of accent in his words, but somehow I knew that he first formulated his reply in Chinese, then laboriously translated each syllable into English before uttering it.

"Who is it we have come to see?" I asked as the servant vanished silently, his footfalls noiseless on the deep-piled rugs as if he walked on sand.

"Doctor Wong Kim Tien, greatest living authority on Mongolian lore and Oriental magic in the world," de Grandin answered soberly. "If he cannot help us——"

"Good Lord, you mean you've dragged me from the bedside of a desperately sick girl to consult a mumbo-jumbo occultist —and a Chinaman in the bargain?" I blazed.

"Not a Chinaman, a Mongol and a Manchu," he corrected.

"Well, what the devil is the difference——"

"The difference between the rabbit and the stoat, *parbleu!* Do you not know history, my friend? Have you not read how this people conquered all the country from Tibet to the Caspian and from the Dnieper to the China Sea—how they laid the castles of the terrible Assassins in heaps of smoking ruins——"

"Who cares what they did before Columbus crossed the ocean? The fact remains we've left a critically ill patient to go gallivanting over the country to consult this faker, and——"

"I would not use such words if I were you, my friend," he warned. "A Manchu's honor is a precious thing and his vanity is very brittle. If you were overheard——"

The messenger's return cut short our budding quarrel. "The Master bids you come," he told us as if he were about to usher us into the presence of some potentate.

We climbed flight after flight of winding stairs, and as we went I was impressed with the fact that the place seemed more a fortress than an ordinary

DR. DE GRANDIN

I HAD no preconceived impression of the man we were to meet, save that he would probably look like any Chinaman, butter-colored, broad-faced, button-nosed, probably immensely fat, and certainly a full head shorter than the average Caucasian.

The man who crossed the room to greet de Grandin was the opposite of my mind's picture. He was exceptionally tall, six feet three, at least, and lean and hard-conditioned as an athlete. Straight, black hair slanted sleekly upward from a high and rather narrow forehead, his nose was large and aquiline, his smooth-shaved lips were thin and firm, his high cheek-bones cased in skin of ruddy bronze, like that of a Sioux Indian. But most of all it was his eyes that fascinated me. Only slightly slanting, they were hooded by low-drooping lids, and were an indeterminate color, slate-gray, perhaps, possibly agate; certainly not black. They were meaningful eyes, knowing, weary, slightly bitter—as if they had seen from their first opening that the world was a tiresome place and that its ever-changing foibles were as meaningless as ripples on a shallow brooklet's surface.

The room in which we stood was as unusual in appearance as its owner. It was thirty feet in length, at least, and occupied the full width of the house. Casement windows, glazed with richly painted glass, looked out upon the roof-tops of the buildings opposite and the festooned backyard clotheslines of the tenements that clustered to the north. Chinese rugs woven when the Son of Heaven bore the surname Ming strewed the polished floors, and the place was warmly lighted by two monster lamps with pierced brass shades. The furniture was oddly mixed, lacquered Chinese pieces mingling with Turkish ottomans like overgrown boudoir pillows, and here and there a bit of Indian cane-ware.

house. Steel doors were everywhere, shutting off the corridors, closing stairheads, making it impossible for anything less potent than a battery of field guns to force a passage from one floor to another, or even from the front to the rear of the building. Thick bars were at each window, and in the ceilings I caught glimpses of ammonia atomizers such as those they have in prisons to subdue unruly convicts. But if the place was strong, it was also lovely. Porcelains, silks, carved jades, choice pieces of the goldsmith's art, were everywhere. Walls were hung with draperies which even I could recognize as priceless, and the rugs we trod must have been well worth their area in treasury notes. Finally, when it seemed to me we had ascended more steps than those leading to the Woolworth Building's tower, our guide came to a halt, held aside a brocade curtain and motioned us to pass through the steel door which had been opened for our coming. De Grandin led the way and we stepped into the study of Doctor Wong Kim Tien.

Book-shelves ran along one wall, bound volumes in every language of the Occident and Orient sharing space with scrolls of silk wound on ivory rods. Other shelves were filled with vases, small and large, with rounding surfaces of cream-colored crackle, or blood-red glaze or green or blue-and-white that threw back iridescent lights like reflections from a softly changing kaleidoscope. Upon a high stand was an aquarium in which swam several goldfish of the most gorgeous coloring I had ever seen, while near the northern windows was a refectory table of old oak littered with chemical apparatus. Glass-sided cases held a startling miscellany—mummified heads and hands and feet, old weapons, ancient tablets marked with cuneiform inscriptions. An articulated skeleton swung from a metal stand and leered at us sardonically.

"*Kungskee-kungskee*, little brother," our host greeted, clasping his hands before his blue-and-yellow robe and bowing to de Grandin, then advancing to shake hands in Western fashion. "What fair wind has brought you here?"

"*Tiens,* I hardly know myself," the little Frenchman answered as he performed the rites of introduction and the Manchu almost crushed my knuckles in a vise-like grip. "It is about a woman that we come, an American young woman who suffered from a seeming lightning-stroke two nights ago and now lies babbling in her bed."

The Manchu doctor smiled at him ironically. "This one is honored that the learned, skilful Jules de Grandin, graduate of the Sorbonne and once professor at the *Ecole Médical de Paris* should seek his humble aid," he murmured. "Have you perhaps administered the usual remedies, given her hypnotics to control her nervousness——"

"*Grand Dieu des artichauts!*" the Frenchman interrupted; "this is no time to jest, my old one. I said a *seeming* lightning-stroke, if you will recall, and if you will attend me carefully I shall show you why it is I seek your so distinguished help."

Quickly he rehearsed the incidents of Sylvia's mishap, recalled the floating ball of fire which struck her down, told of her vision of the Orient city; finally, dramatically: "Now she lies and murmurs, '*Oom mani padme—oom mani padme!*'" he concluded. "Am I, or am I not, entitled to your counsel?"

"My little one, you are!" the other answered. "Wait while I change my clothes and I will go at once to see this girl who chants the Buddhist litany in her delirium, yet has never been outside this country."

Arrayed in tweeds and Panama the Oriental savant joined us in a little while and we set out for Sylvia Dearborn's.

"What is that chant she keeps repeating?" I asked as we left the tunnel and started on the road across the meadows.

"'*Oom mani padme*' is literally 'Hail the Jewel of the Lotus,' Doctor Wong replied, "but actually it has far more significance than its bare translation into English would suggest. Gautama Siddgartha, or Buddha, as you know him, is generally shown as seated in a giant lotus blossom, you know, and for that reason is poetically referred to as the Jewel of the Lotus. But this phrase of worship has acquired a special significance through countless repetitions. It is the constant prayer of the devout Buddhist, it is inscribed on his sacred banners and on his prayer wheels, and one 'acquires merit'—something like obtaining an indulgence in the Roman Catholic faith—by constantly repeating it. To the followers of Buddha it is like the *Allah Akbar* to the Mohammedan or the *Gloria Patri* to the Christian. It is, at once praise and prayer in all Buddhistic ceremonies, and with it they are all begun and ended. For a Buddhist to say it is as natural as to draw his breath, but for an American young lady, especially of such narrow background as your patient's, to begin intoning it is more than merely strange; it is incredible, perhaps indicative of something very dreadful."

THE morphine torpor was relinquishing its hold on Sylvia when we reached her. From time to time she rolled her head upon the pillow, moaning like a person who dreams dreadful dreams. Once or twice she seemed about to speak, but only thick-tongued sounds proceeded from her mouth. De Grandin tiptoed to the window and raised the blind to bring the patient's face in clearer definition and as the lances of bright sunlight slanted sharply down upon the bed the girl rose to a sitting posture, flung out her arms as though to ward off an assailant and cried out in a voice honed sharp with fear, "No, no, I tell you; I won't let you! You can't have me! I won't——" As suddenly as it had commenced, her outburst ceased, and she fell back on the pillows, breathing with the heavy, gasping respiration of one totally exhausted.

De Grandin bent and rearranged the bed-clothes. "You see?" he asked the Manchu. "She suffers from the fixed idea that someone or some *thing* seeks to enter in her—*grand Dieu*, it comes again, *l'extase perverse!* Behold her, how she metamorphosizes!"

A subtle change had come into the young girl's face. The corners of her eyes went up, her mouth drooped at the corners, and her firmly molded lips appeared to swell and thicken. A sly, triumphant smile spread across her altered countenance, and she roused again, glancing sidewise at us with a cunning leer.

"*Empad inam moo!*" she exclaimed suddenly, for all the world like a naughty child who giggles a forbidden phrase. "*Empad inam moo!*" But the voice that spoke the singsong words was never hers. It was a high, cracked tone, like the utterance of an adolescent whose voice has not quite finished changing, or the treble of a senile graybeard, but it was definitely masculine.

"*Dor-je-tshe-ring!*" Doctor Wong exclaimed, and:

"*Kilao yeh hsieh ti to lo!*" that alien voice replied ironically, speaking through the girl's fast-thickening lips as a ventriloquist might make his words appear to issue from his dummy's painted mouth.

Doctor Wong addressed a very diatribe of hissing gutturals at the girl, and she answered with a flow of singsong syllables, shaking her head, grinning at him with a sly malevolence. They seemed to be in deadly argument, Wong urging something with great earnestness, Sylvia replying with cool irony, as though she were defying him.

At last the Manchu turned away. "Renew the opiate, my friend," he ordered wearily. "It will not last as long this time, but while she is unconscious she will rest. Afterward"—he smiled a hard-lipped smile—"we shall see what can be done."

"You have a plan of treatment?" I inquired.

"I have," he answered earnestly, "and unless it is successful it would be much better that you made this dose of morphine fatal."

The girl fought like a tigress when we tried to give her the narcotic. Scratching, biting, screaming imprecations in that strange heathen tongue, she beat us off repeatedly with the frenzied strength of madness, and it was not until they fairly hurled themselves upon her and held her fast that I was able to administer the morphine. This time the drug worked slowly, and almost an hour had elapsed before we saw her eyelids droop and she sank into a troubled sleep.

"I think it would be well if we secured two nurses used to handling the insane," advised de Grandin as we quit our bedside vigil. "It would be nothing less than murder to administer another dose of morphine after this; yet she must be protected from herself and we cannot remain here. We have important duties to perform elsewhere."

I telephoned the agency and in less than half an hour two stout females who looked as if they might be champion wrestlers in their leisure time reported at the Dearborn home. "*Pipe d'un chameau!*" de Grandin chuckled as he viewed our new recruits; "I damn think Mademoiselle Sylvia will have more trouble with those ones than she had with Doctor Wong and me, should she take a notion to go walking in our absence!"

Instructions given to the nurses, we set out once more for New York, Wong and de Grandin talking earnestly in whispers,

I with a feeling I had blundered inadvertently into a fairy-tale, or come upon a modern version of the Mad Hatter's tea party.

LUNCHEON waited at the house in Chinatown and was served by Doctor Wong's diminutive factotum, who had changed his black-silk uniform for a short jacket of bright red worn above a skirt of blue, both embroidered in large circles of lotus flowers around centers of conventional good-fortune designs. The meal consisted of a clear soup in which boiled chestnuts and dice of apple floated, followed by stewed shellfish and mushrooms, steamed shark fin served with ham and crabmeat, roast duck stuffed with young pine needles, preserved pomegranates and plums, finally small cups of rice wine. Throughout the courses our cups of steaming, fragrant jasmine tea were never allowed to be more than half empty.

"A question, *mon ami*," de Grandin asked as he raised his thrice-replenished cup of rice wine; "what was it Mademoiselle Dearborn said when first the change came on her? It sounded like——"

"It was the anagram of '*Oom mani padme—empad inam moo.*'" Doctor Wong's words were crisp and brittle, without a trace of accent. "To say it in a Buddhist's presence is gratuitous sacrilege, much like repeating a Christian prayer backward, as the witches of the Middle Ages were supposed to do when meeting for their sabbats. It is the *hong* or sign manual of certain heretical Buddhist sects, notably those who have blended the *Bon-Pal*, or ancient devil-worship of Tibet, with Buddhist teachings."

"And what was it you said to her?" I asked.

Doctor Wong broke the porcelain stopper from a teapot-shaped container of *n'gapi* and decanted a double-thimbleful of the potent, amber-colored liquid into his cup before he answered. "Buddhism, Doctor Trowbridge, is like every other old religion. It far outdates Christianity, you know, and for that reason has had just that many more centuries in which to acquire incrustations of heresy. Like Christianity and Mohammedanism, it has been preached around the world, and its convents number millions. But the old gods die hard. Indeed, I think it might be said they never truly die; they merely change their names. Exactly as one may see survivals of the deities of ancient Rome none too thickly veiled in the pantheon of Christian saints, or discern strong vestiges of Gallic Druidism in the pow-wows and Hex practises of the Pennsylvania yokels, so the informed observer has no difficulty in seeing the ill-favored visages of the savage elder gods peering through the fabric of many heretical Buddhist sects. Some of these are harmless, as the Maryology of certain sects of Christians is. Some are extremely mischievous, as was the grafting of demonolatry on mediæval Christianity, with witchcraft persecutions, heresy huntings and other bloody consequences."

He lit an amber-scented cigarette, almost as long and thick as a cigar, and blew a cloud of fragrant smoke toward the red-and-gold ceiling, looking quizically at me through the drifting wreaths. "You know the Khmers?"

"Never heard of them," I confessed.

His thin lips drew back in a smile, and little wrinkles formed against the ruddy-yellow skin stretched tight across his temples, but his heavy-hooded eyes retained their look of brooding speculation. "I should have strongly doubted your veracity if you had answered otherwise," he told me frankly.

"Long ago, so long that archeologists have refused to place the time, there boiled up out of India one of those strange migrations which have marked Asia since the first tick on the clock of time. It was a people on the march; across the lowlands, up the foothills, over the dragon-toothed mountains they came, kings with their elephants, priests in their golden carts, warriors a-horseback, the common people trudging arm to arm with their goods and chattels and their household gods in bundles on their backs. They swarmed across broad rivers, splashed neck-deep through marshes, crashed through the darkness of the matted jungle land. And finally they came to rest in that part of lower Asia which we call Cambodia today. There they built a mighty nation. They raised great cities in the jungle waste—not only Angkor Thom, their capital, which had a population of a million and a half—but other towns of brick and stone, stretching clear across the Cambodian peninsula. Brahmanism was their state religion, and the temples which they built to Siva the Destroyer are the puzzle and despair of modern archeologists. Later—sometime in the Fifth Century as the West reckons time—missionaries came preaching the religion of the Lord Gautama, and Buddhism became the chief faith in the land. But the old gods die hard, Doctor Trowbridge. While images of Buddha replaced the Siva idols in the temples the philosophy of Buddha did not replace Brahmanism in the people's hearts, and the old religion mingled with and fouled the new system. In their sculpture they show the Lord Gautama seated side by side with the seven-headed cobra; some of their ornamental friezes show whole rows of Buddhas carrying a giant serpent. It was a degenerate and schismatic sect that flourished in the jungle."

HE PAUSED and helped himself daintily to another stoup of rice wine. Then:

"Two hundred years after Indian missionaries had preached the doctrines of the Buddha to the Khmers, other zealous bonzes penetrated far Tibet. The new faith took quick root, but it was like the seed that fell on stony ground in your Gospel parable. Pure Buddhism could not flourish into blossom in those devil-haunted uplands of the Himalayas. The thing which finally grew was a superstitious system which resembled Indian and Chinese Buddhism about as closely as the hierarchy of the Abyssinian Orthodox Church did the Twelve Apostles who followed your great teacher. With its crude admixture of the Bon-Pal of ancient Tibet and degenerate Buddhism, it is almost pure demonolatry, and the outgrowth of it is that queer system known as Lamaism. Sacrilegiously— when everything is taken into account— the leading lamas please to call themselves Buddhas, and centuries ago the doctrine that the Buddha never dies, but is reincarnated in his priests and lamas from one generation to another, was announced.

"There is more than one 'Living Buddha.' Besides the Dalai Lama of Tibet there are several 'living gods' in outer Mongolia, all lineal descendants of the Lord Gautama through infant-reincarnation."

"Infant-reincarnation?" I echoed, mystified.

"Exactly. As each successive Living Buddha falls into his final illness, subordinate lamas seek a fitting substitute in some infant born at the time the Living Buddha breathes his last, and into the body of the new-born child the soul of Buddha passes. So, according to tradition, it has been passed and repassed for countless generations.

"But there was among the ancient lamas a man who did not wish to have his soul incorporated in the new flesh of a whimpering infant; who did not want to start life with no recollection of his former incarnation, and this man, named 'The Thunderbolt'—Dor-je-tshe-ring in the Tibetan—decided to develop magic powers whereby he could pass consciously into the body of a living adult person, crowd out the other's soul—or consciousness or personality, whichever term you choose—and continue living with the full retention of his faculties and in the vigor of young manhood. It came about as close to immortality as any earthly thing could, you see."

"I should say so, if it could be worked."

"It could, and has. There is ample testimony in the ancient records that he did it not once but many times. Nor was it merely poetry that named him Thunderbolt. When he was about to expire from one body, the records tell us, his soul was seen to issue from his lips in the form of a small ball of fire, and pass from his old body to the new one. The body of the person struck by this fiery ball at once collapsed, with every evidence of being struck by lightning. Sometimes it would struggle, as if it had been seized with nervous spasms, but eventually these fits of resistance passed, and when they did, the stricken body spoke with Dor-je-tshe-ring's voice, acted as he had in his former fleshy habitation and, to a great degree, assumed his facial aspects.

"Tibet is superstition-ridden and the sorcerers and lamas can do things there no other country would permit, but it appears the Thunderbolt became unbearable even there; so with a thousand vengeful hillmen in pursuit, he fled down to the lowlands of Cambodia where, sometime in the period corresponding to the Western calendar's Eighth Century, he appeared in all his glory, having assumed the body of the reigning Buddhist dignitary as his own. Dor-je-tshe-ring was probably the foremost heretic of his day. He was among the earliest, if not the very first, to institute recital of Oom mani padme in reverse—offering conscious and intended insult to the Buddha by chanting Empad inam moo at Buddhist ceremonies.

"He ruled high-handedly in Angkor Thom for many years, and—this is believed by many historians—it was he who led them to oblivion. However that may be, the fact remains that the disappearance of the Khmers is one of the great mysteries of all time. There they were, a mighty nation with a high degree of culture, owners of proud cities, populous and powerful. Then one day, as abruptly and mysteriously as they came, they vanished. Their crowded cities were left empty as a tomb despoiled by grave-robbers, their market-places were deserted, their sanctuaries had no priests to serve them. Overnight, apparently, the Khmer Empire, the Khmer culture, the entire Khmer nation, disappeared. They did not die. Explorers have found no skeletal remains to evidence a plague or widespread massacre in their great, empty cities. They simply vanished, and the tiger and the lizard occupied their courts, the jungle flowed back to their streets and squares and palaces and temples."

"Quite so, but what's all this to do with Sylvia Dearborn?" I asked.

"Everything, by blue!" de Grandin answered quickly. "Tell him, mon vieux —tell him what you told me of the Khmer capital!"

Doctor Wong inclined his head. "Doctor de Grandin is correct," he nodded. "I think there is a strong connection. You recall Miss Dearborn's telling you about her vision of an ancient Oriental city? Her description closely parallels that of a countryman of mine, Tcheou-Ta-Quan, who was ambassador to Angkor Thom in the early Thirteenth Century."

Going to a lacquered bookcase he took down a slim volume bound in vellum, thumbed through its crackling parchment pages, and began to read:

"When the king of Angkor leaves his palace he moves with a troop of horsemen at the head of his column. After the guard of cavalry are standard-bearers with fluttering flags, and behind them march the music-makers. Next in the procession are hundreds of concubines and girls of the palace . . . after them are other women of the palace carrying objects of gold and silver. Following them are the men-at-arms, the soldiers of the palace guard. In their wake come chariots and royal carriages all of gold and drawn by bulls. Behind these are the elephants in which ride nobles and ministers of the government. Each rides beneath a red umbrella.

"In carriages or golden chairs or thrones borne on the backs of elephants are the wives and favorite concubines of the king, and their parasols are golden.

"The king himself comes last, standing on an elephant and holding in his hand the sacred sword, while soldiers riding elephants or horses crowd closely by his side as he proceeds through the city.

"THE similarity between Miss Dearborn's vision and Tcheou-Ta-Quan's description of a state procession in the Khmer capital is very close, and when it is remembered that the Living Buddha of Angkor occupied an ecclesiastical position analogous to that of the Archbishop of Canterbury, if not quite as exalted as that of mediæval Popes, the meaning of her vision is quite plain. In my mind there is no doubt that through the eyes of Dor-je-tshe-ring she watched a ceremonial procession in which the king and his retinue marched through Angkor Thom to do their Living Buddha honor. That accounts for her saying 'one part of me seemed to understand it, while the other didn't', and also for her feeling of a dual personality, as if she were man and woman in one body."

"'You see?" de Grandin asked.

"I don't think——"

W. T.—1

44

"Then in heaven's name, do not boast of it, my friend. Cannot you understand? How else could this American young lady, this girl who never in her life had been to Europe, much less to lower Asia, behold that ceremonial march of ghosts from a long-forgotten past? This never-sufficiently-to-be-deprecated old one has struck down Mademoiselle Dearborn with his 'thunderbolt' and has entered into her. He is forcing forth her mind, he is making her assume the features of his so vile monkey-face; he is leaving her a living body while he kills her soul!"

"But how could he come over here, and why should he assume a woman's body? I thought the Living Buddha always is a man——"

Doctor Wong smiled frostily. " 'The best-laid schemes of mice and men gang aft a-gley," he quoted. "According to the ancient chronicles his soul in fire-ball form passed seven times about the earth with the speed of sound before it struck the body of his victim. We do not know where Dor-je-tshe-ring's former body was when physical death took place, but we may allow for some deviation in his calculations. Instead of returning to China, or Manchukuo, or perhaps Korea or Siam, where his expiring body lay, his malignant spirit came to rest on that hotel rooftop in New Jersey. He may have been disconcerted by this happening, or, more probably, he intended to strike down the nearest masculine body to his place of rest, but through another error in his calculations, he struck Miss Dearborn's body instead. There seems to be a definite limit to his power. Once before he made an error; that time he entered the body of a cripple, and as he could not leave his earthly tenement till natural death ensued, he led the poor, unfortunate bit of deformed flesh a miserable dance until he literally wore it out. Then
W. T.—2

he was able to transfer his headquarters to a home more suited to his wishes."

"But certainly," de Grandin seconded. "Our learned friend knew all these things, and being a mathematician as well as a philosopher, he found that two and two made four when added. Accordingly he damn suspected that the finger of this execrable Dor-je-tshe-ring was in the pie up to the elbow, and when he heard the poor young woman reciting Buddhist invocations in reverse, he taxed the villain with his act of trespass, calling him by name. And what was it he said? 'Ki lao yeh hsieh ti to lo,—the honorable gentleman has my thanks,' by dammit. The sixty-times-accursed scoundrel not only admitted his so vile identity, he thanked our friend for recognizing him!"

My senses whirled from their wild talk no less than from the unfamiliar rice wine. "If what you say is true," I asked, "how are we to call back Sylvia's wandering spirit and expel this other from her?"

"That is for Doctor Wong to say," de Grandin answered.

"That is for me to try," the Oriental amended. "I will do the best I can. Whether I succeed or fail is for whatever gods may be to say. If you have completed luncheon, we can begin to make our preparations, gentlemen."

WONG'S apparatus was assembled quickly. At his sharply-spoken order the servant brought a slab of lucent, polished jade from one of the tall lacquered cabinets and laid it on the long refectory table. It must have been of priceless value, for it was at least a foot in length by a full eight inches wide, and certainly not less than one inch thick. Going to a locked steel chest Wong took a tiny phial of bright ruby glass, spilled a single drop of amber fluid from it on the slab of jade and began to polish it with a wad of gleaming yellow silk. As he rubbed the oil across the jade slab's gleaming face there crept through the room a perfume of an almost nameless sweetness, so rich and heady that my senses fairly reeled with it. For perhaps five minutes he worked silently, then, apparently satisfied, laid his silken buffer by and wrapped the jade block in a bolt of violet tissue.

In a tall, glass-fronted case stood a row of ancient bottles, fragile objects of exquisite delicacy, flat-bodied, small-mouthed, each with a tiny spoon attached to its stopper. One of shadowed malachite, one of glowing amber, one of richly-gleaming coral he lifted from their shelves, and from each he scooped a minute portion of fine powder, stirred them carefully with a thin amber rod, then dusted them into a phial of gray agate and closed the bottle-neck with a rock crystal plug.

Finally, while the servant brought a Buddhist prayer wheel with disk of polished silver and uprights of age-black poplar wood, he took two tall, thick candles of blue wax set in crystal standards, wrapped them in a length of silken tissue, drew a censer of antique red gold from its case of cinnabar and ivory, and nodded to us.

"If you are quite ready, let us go," he suggested courteously.

"**H**AS she rested quietly, *Mademoiselle?*" de Grandin asked the more feminine-looking of the amazonian nurses when we arrived at Sylvia's room.

"Yes, sir, mostly. Once or twice she's been delirious, muttering and groaning, but she really hasn't given us much trouble."

"Thank you," he responded with a bow. "Now if you and your companion will await us in the hall, we shall begin our treatment. Come quickly if we call, but on no account come in the room or permit anyone else to enter till we give the word."

They made their preparations quickly. Sylvia's bed was moved until her head lay to the west and her feet east, that she might receive the natural magnetic currents of the earth. They stripped her green pajamas off, anointed her forehead, breasts, hands and feet with some pungently sweet-smelling oil, then crossed her hands upon her bosom, the right one uppermost, and bound her wrists together with a length of purple silk, that she might not change her posture. Her slender ankles were then crossed as they had crossed her wrists, and bound firmly with a red-silk sash. Beneath her head they put a pillow of bright-yellow silk embroidered with a swastika design in black. At one side of the bed they set the jade slab upright, and across from it they stood the dark-blue candles with the silver prayer wheel behind them. Doctor Wong filled the golden censer from the agate bottle, snapped a very modern cigarette-lighter into flame, lit the candles and set the incense glowing.

The scented smoke filled the room as wine may fill a bottle, penetrating every cranny, every crevice, every nook, sinking deep into the rugs and draperies, billowing and rolling back from walls and ceiling. It was curiously and pungently sweet, yet lacked the heavy, cloying fragrance of the usual incense.

They had drawn the blinds and pulled the curtains to, and the only light within the chamber came from the two tall candles which burned straight-flamed in the unwavering air, sending their yellow rays to beat upon the mirror-lustered surface of the slab of jade.

De Grandin put his hand upon the prayer wheel and at a word from Wong began to spin its disk. Astonishingly, the polished silver of the whirling disk caught up the candle rays, focused them as a lens will focus sunlight, and shot them back in a single sword-straight ray against the slab of glowing jade. Queerly, too, although he did not move the wheel's base, the beam of light moved up and down and crosswise on the jade mirror; then, as though it were a liquid stream, it seemed to ebb and flow as moonlight spreads on gently-running water.

Doctor Wong was chanting in a low, monotonous voice, long, singsong words which rose and fell and seemed to slip and glide into one another until his canticle was more like a continuous flow of sound than words and sentences and phrases.

The nude girl on the bed stirred restlessly. She sought to take her hands down from her bosom, to uncross her feet, but the bandages prevented, and she lapsed back in what seemed a quiet sleep.

The long-drawn, uninflected chant proceeded, and the incense thickened in the room until I felt that I was being smothered. Where the prayer wheel whirled there came a low, monotonous humming, something like the droning hum made by an electric fan, but more penetrating, more insistent. It seemed to come from earth and air and sky, from the walls themselves, and to fill the atmosphere to overflowing with a spate of quivering sound that tore the nerves to tatters, shattering all inhibitions and dredging up dark memories and hates from the murk of the subconscious mind. I felt that I was going mad, that in another instant I should scream and tear my garments, or fall driveling and mouthing to the floor, when the sudden change in Sylvia's face caught and centered my attention.

Something alien had flowed into her

features. Atop the perfect, cream-white body lying bound upon the bed was another face, an old face, a wicked face, a face with Mongoloid features steeped and sodden in foul malice.

A whining child-moan trickled from the thickening lips; then with a scream of fear surcharged with hatred she sat up struggling on the bed, tearing at the bonds that held her wrists, fighting like a thing possessed against the bandages that held her long, slim feet crossed on each other. But the silken fetters held— they had been tied with seven knots and sealed with red wax stamped with the ideograph of Lord Gautama!

And the low, monotonous chant went on, the incense foamed and frothed and billowed through the room, the gleaming candlelight pulsed throbbingly against the jade reflector, the silver wheel whirled on, giving off its nerve-destroying murmur.

"Grand Dieu!" I heard de Grandin's whisper rasping through the whirring of the wheel. "Observe her—look, Friend Trowbridge, he comes; he is emerging!"

Wearied by her futile struggles, Sylvia had fallen back upon the bed, and as her head sank flaccidly upon the black-embroidered yellow pillow, from her mouth, squared in a scream, there came a flow of luminance. Yet it was not merely light, it was a shining thing of ponderable substance, swelling as it reached the air till it hung above her face like a pear-shaped phosphorescent bubble joined to her by a single gossamer thread of fiery brilliance.

Idiotically—like a nervous woman tittering at a funeral—I giggled. More than anything else the dreadful tableau reminded me of a conjurer disgorging the collapsible property egg he has pretended to swallow.

The beam reflected from the swiftly whirling prayer wheel's silver disk cut athwart her face and, as if it had been a sharpened sword, clipped the ligature of luminance tethering the pyriform excrescence to her lips.

The brightly-glowing globe seemed to shrink in upon itself, to acquire added weight and solidarity, yet oddly to become more buoyant. For an instant it hovered in midair above her face, as though undecided which way it should float; then, suddenly, like an iron-filing drawn to a strong magnet, it dropped upon the light-beam slanting from the prayer wheel to the plinth of jade and slid along the lucent track like a brakeless motor car gone headlong down a hill.

The impact was terrific. The jade rang like a smitten gong, a dreadful clang of sound, a shrill, high, wailing note as though it—or the ball of luminosity—had cried out in mortal anguish, a note of tortured outcry that thinned and lengthened to a sickening scream of torment. It hung and quivered in the incense-saturated air for what seemed an eternity, until I could not say if I still heard it or if tortured ear-drums held it in remembrance, and would go on remembering it till madness wiped the recollection out.

The jade was shattered in a thousand slivered fragments and the light-globe was dissolved in vapor thin as cirrous clouds that race before the rushing stormwind, and blended with the hovering brume of incense. But a foul odor, rank and sickening as the fetor from decaying flesh, spread through the room, blotting out the perfume of the incense, bringing tears to our eyes and retchings to our stomachs.

"*Barbe bleu,* he had the fragrance of the rotten fish, that one!" exclaimed de Grandin as he raced across the room to fling the windows open and began to fan the air with a bath towel.

I looked at Sylvia. The invading presence had withdrawn and her lovely features were composed and calm. She lay there flaccidly, only the light flutter of her bosom telling us she was alive. I took her wrist between my thumb and forefinger. Her pulse was striking eighty clear-cut beats a minute. Normal. She was well.

THEY cut the silken bandages from wrists and ankles, drew her green pajamas on and tucked her in beneath the bed-clothes. Then, while I went to order broth and brandy ready for her waking, Wong and de Grandin packed their apparatus in its soft silk swaddling-clothes, swept up the bits of shattered jade and drew their chairs up to the bedside.

We sat beside her till the dawnlight blushed across the eastern sky and day, advancing, trod upon the heels of night.

With the coming of the day she wakened. She lay against the heaped-up pillows, warm, relaxed and faintly smiling. One arm was underneath her head and the attitude showed her lines of gracious femininity; charming, tenderly and softly curved. Against the whiteness of the pillows and the counterpane her copper hair and fresh-blown cheeks glowed like an apricot that ripens in the sun.

But when she sat up with a sudden start her lovely color drained away and violet semicircles showed beneath her eyes. The glint of waking laughter that had kindled in her face was stilled and we could see fear flooding in her glance as blood wells through a sodden bandage. She licked dry lips with a tongue that had gone stiff, and her hands fluttered to her mouth in the immemorial, unconscious gesture of a woman sick with mortal terror. "Oh"—she began, and we heard the hot breath press against her words, as if her laboring heart were forcing it against them—"I thought——"

"Do not attempt to do so, *Mademoiselle*," de Grandin told her with firm gentleness. "You have been severely ill; this is no time for thought, unless you wish to think of getting well all soon, and of the one who comes tonight—*eh bien*, my little pigeon, have I not seen it in his eyes? But certainly! Drink this, if you please; then compose yourself to think of Monsieur Georges and the pretty compliments that he will whisper when he sees you lying here so beautiful —and filled to overflowing with returning strength. But certainly; yes, of course!"

WE PAUSED upon the Dearborn porch, weary with our vigil, but happy with the happiness of men who see their plans succeed. "How did you do it——" I began, but de Grandin cut my question off half uttered.

"Those things of Doctor Wong's were ancient things—and good things," he explained. "For more generations than the three of us have hairs upon our heads they have served the good of mankind— the sacred incense from the very tree beneath which Buddha sat in contemplation, the oil with which the Emperors of China were anointed, the clear, pellucid jade that casts back only good reflections, the candles made from wax of bees that drew their nectar in the very fields in which Gautama walked and preached, and last of all the prayer wheel that has recorded countless holy men's devout petitions to the Lord of Good—call Him what you will, He is the same in every heart filled with the love of man, whatever name He bears.

"Against these things, and against the ancient formulæ our friend Wong chanted, the evil one was powerless. *Parbleu*, they drew him forth from her as one withdraws the fish of April from the brooklet with a hook!"

"But," I ventured doubtfully, "isn't there a chance he may come back to plague——"

"I hardly think so," Doctor Wong replied. "He smashed the sacred mirror of *pi yü*—jade, that is—but in breaking it he also broke himself. You smelled the stench? That was his evil spirit vanishing. For almost countless generations he had occupied the flesh, first in one body, then another. Dissolution—putrefaction —was long in overtaking him, but at last it sought him out. No, Doctor Trowbridge, I think the world has seen the last of Dor-je-tshe-ring, 'The Thunderbolt.' He has struck down his last victim, he has sucked in his last——"

"*Morbleu*, I am reminded by your reference to the sucking in!" de Grandin interrupted as he glanced at the small watch strapped on his wrist.

We looked at him in wonder. "Of what are you reminded, little brother?" asked Doctor Wong.

"In fifteen little minutes they will open. If we hurry, we can be among the first!"

"The first? What is it that you want?"

"Three, four, perhaps half a dozen of those magnificent old-fashioned cocktails; those with the so lovely whisky in them. Come, let us hasten!"

Dread Summons

By PAUL ERNST

The old butler heard a scream, muffled by the street noises from outside, and when he investigated he found that a dread summons had been answered

HERB MELLER stared at the great house on Chicago's chief boulevard with a grim and savage pride, the house that had once belonged to that bleak old financier, R. J. Hill.

The structure was six stories tall, containing nearly forty rooms. It was a palace; built thirty years before at a cost of over two million dollars; situated now on land so valuable that if it were covered with gold pieces the sum would hardly approximate its worth.

A palace! One of the costliest buildings in Chicago! Yet it was but a fraction of what Meller had wrested from the Hill estate. He had looted millions from the fortune of the ferocious old man who had taken so long in dying. This house on the boulevard faded into insignificance when compared to the total.

Yet for Herbert Meller it was a symbol, and its possession gave him more exultation than all the rest. The very citadel and personal pride of old Hill had been won when he took that house away from Hill's spinster daughter.

Meller walked from the sidewalk to the great flags leading up to the door of the palace. He stared with swelling approval of himself at the ponderous iron grillework of the front door.

Born on the wrong side of the tracks, eh? Well, he'd shown Hill and all his crew. Since Meller had been ten years old he had paused before this place, on his way to swim naked in the lake with other grubby little slum urchins, and looked at that great iron door. He couldn't have entered the huge Hill house even by the back door in those days. Now—he owned the place.

There was a thrill in finding the key to the house on his fat key-ring. "I don't know that you'll want to bother looking into the old mausoleum," the agent had said, giving him the key, "as long as it is to be torn down so soon anyway."

But he *had* wanted to look through it. In a week, men would be here to dismantle the house, which had become a positive liability through the years, a worthless lump of stone and splendor on an invaluable site. A hotel corporation had bought the place for that site. The Hill home was only in the way.

He inserted the key in the massive lock. Imported from Italy, the iron grillework of the door had been. Old Hill had spread himself on his house.

"Much good it did him!" Meller spat viciously as he worked with the key.

Meller always saw red when he thought of the grim, hard old man. A blatant pusher, a cheap gambler, Hill had called Meller. The old man had refused steadily to have anything to do with the ruthless young fellow who was springing so far and so swiftly from the slums. "Damned young slug," the old man had said once—to his face. And Meller had never forgotten nor forgiven the reference to his soft fat, the result of having

50

"The door moved a little against his hand, moved slightly, eerily."

no time off from business for the less important task of keeping himself fit. Well, he had wiped out all insults. . . .

THE door suddenly opened as he was fiddling with the key. An old man, at least seventy, dressed in a plain blue serge suit faced him in the doorway. The blue serge made his thin hair seem even whiter and his faded blue eyes appear even more faded.

Meller was startled for a moment. Then he remembered that the old Hill butler had volunteered to stay on as caretaker till the place was torn down. For

nothing! The old fool! Anyone that worked without fat rewards was an idiot, in Herb Meller's estimation.

"Yes, sir?" the butler quavered, inquiringly.

"I'm Meller."

The announcement made no impression.

"The man who owns this house now," Meller said impatiently.

"Oh! Oh, yes, sir. And you want to look around?"

Meller nodded and pushed his way in. He was shorter than the old servant; a short fat man who, even at forty-one, puffed a little as he walked and perspired freely from a fat, rather apoplectic-looking countenance.

"Shall I direct you, sir?" said the butler.

"No." Meller clipped it out harshly. "Get out of here. I can find my own way around, I guess."

"Very good, sir. There is the elevator."

He pointed with a gnarled old hand to an automatic cage at the rear of the front hall. And Meller almost snarled as he gazed at that. An elevator in a private home! In the home he'd been raised in there hadn't even been a bathroom or electricity.

"All right," he said, more to himself than to the servant. He walked toward the elevator, meanwhile looking at the hall of this home in which he would once have been treated as dirt but which was now his—at least till the hotel people tore it down.

The great front hall was as lofty as a church nave. In a way it had the same kind of hushed atmosphere. It made Meller feel small as his hard heels rapped across the polished parquet floor.

He tapped irritably at the floor with his cane. The wood was as ornate, as beautifully inlaid as a table-top. It woke savage hate in him. The ferrule of his stick was of metal and scuffed to a sharp rim around the edge. He dug deep with the ferrule and then dragged the cane after him.

A great raw scratch resulted in the softly polished, lovely wood. Behind him, Meller heard the old servant gasp as though he had been struck.

"What the hell?" said Meller harshly. "The joint's coming down soon anyway."

He made more scratches, as if he had his stick in the face of old Hill himself. He spelled his name in raw tears in the inlaid wood, laughing as he did so. Then he went on to the elevator.

An elevator in a private house! It still annoyed him, particularly such a little jewel-case as this mahogany and rosewood cage that bore him silently up toward the second floor at a touch of his finger.

There was gilt inlay in the panels. He amused himself by scratching some of it out with his stick on the way up. Then the cage stopped. He opened the door and stepped into a second-floor hall which was smaller than the first-floor reception hall but even more luxurious. The floor was of marble, as were the curving stairs up from the first floor. The marble was bare. The interminable, specially woven strip of oriental carpeting that had padded the staircase and stretched down the corridor had been sold by Hill's daughter along with the other furnishings. Meller's heels rang as he walked down it.

Rooms! An acre of rooms! But he wasn't going to go through all of them. He only wanted to see the suites belonging to old Hill and the wife whose death had been such a shock to him, and the daughter who was now virtually penniless as the result of Meller's clever manipulations. Those three master suites were on this floor.

He walked into the door opposite the elevator cage. He entered what seemed an entire apartment, but eventually resolved itself into two great rooms, with alcoves resulting from the Victorian architecture which was the characteristic of the place. Two huge rooms. One a bedroom, done in dark ivory with walnut trim, opening onto a vast and masculine-looking bath; the other a paneled living-room and library.

This was old Hill's suite. The very air breathed of the bitter old man who till his death had held his associates and enemies, particularly his enemies, in awe of him.

Hill's home had been his love, his fortress. This two-room suite had been the heart of the home, inviolate from all trespassing, dedicated to the fierce non-agenarian who had wrung from a world of smoke and blood and grime the great fortune that had melted at his death.

Hill's holy of holies. And now Meller, the man Hill had held in such contempt, was in here—owned it and all around it.

Meller laughed. There was a mirror on one wall from floor to ceiling. He walked to it, and laughed again. Then his cane lashed out viciously. Thick, that mirror. Quadruple plate. Built to last, as all Hill's things were. It took three ringing cracks before the mirror broke. Then it fairly cascaded to the floor, making a great clatter on the inlaid wood.

THE house seemed as still as a tomb when the clatter ceased. In the silence Meller stood with a funny feeling in the pit of his paunch. He felt a little afraid, somehow. It was his mirror to break if he pleased. It might as well be broken now as later when the house was ripped down.

And yet, he felt—well, funny.

He could almost see Hill coming toward him from the bedroom, grizzled eyebrows drawn together in the savage knot that had made so many tremble. A tyrannical, powerful, frightening old man. A thing of granite, terrible in his icy rages. In life, Meller himself had been afraid of him. He'd admit that. . . .

Meller's too-plump shoulders straightened. No, he wouldn't admit it. By God, he hadn't been afraid of old Hill. That time the old man had figuratively thrown him out of his office by simply walking toward him, while Meller retreated step by step from his blazing eyes—he hadn't

been afraid of Hill, he had simply shown him the respect any younger man gives an old one. The time Hill had almost gotten every cent Meller owned in the steel mill deal——

Meller snarled. Well, Hill had died before that went through. And now he had Hill's hide! Or rather the hide Hill had bequeathed to the dreamy-eyed, silly, retiring woman of forty-five who was his daughter.

Meller turned to the near wall. In a gesture that was childish, though it did not occur to him as being such, he spat on the immaculate cream surface, like the little foul-mouthed, milk-stealing gutter urchin he had once been. With satisfaction he watched the smearing trickle that resulted; watched it spatter slowly down on the fragments of mirror.

Seven years' bad luck, the mirror was supposed to represent. But he wasn't superstitious. He didn't believe in such junk.

He left the rooms that were like an empty shell waiting only for the return of their grim master, and went to the next apartment.

Two rooms here, too. All in pink. Must have been Hill's wife's rooms. Yes, there was a picture of the old boy on a wall between two great windows. The sale hadn't taken in this picture, probably because it was intrinsically worthless. An oil painting, of the old man's head, about eighteen inches square.

Meller laughed again and thrust the ferrule of his stick slowly through the canvas till the wall stopped it. He thrust the metal through the old man's nose—that formidable beak that had matched in jutting power his craggy old jaw. Then he went on to the third suite on this side of the hall; a suite the door of which was just at the head of the great marble staircase.

This was in French gray with silver

trim. It too had been a woman's apartment; but the apartment of a younger woman. It took no subtle intuition to read that. It had belonged without doubt to Hill's daughter.

Meller visioned the daughter. A woman, but so sheltered from life by a doting father that she was no more knowledgable than a girl of eighteen. A person so sensitive and shy and retiring that she was almost a hermit. That was why she had never married, probably. Well, too damned bad for her. Should have a husband to support her now. Meller doubted if she would have fifty dollars a month out of the wreck he had made of her father's fortune.

Meller grinned. The daughter, Beatrice Hill, had actually sought him out for financial advice. Hill's lawyer, that old spider Macy, was responsible for that. After a fat bribe, he had told the daughter that Meller was to be trusted implicitly, that Meller had become Hill's closest associate just before his death.

So Beatrice Hill had come like a damned fool to her father's bitterest enemy. For advice! Well, he'd given her advice. He had shifted worthless securities on her in carload lots. Then he had made loans when her inherited fortune seemed to be in danger. Then, when the worthless securities he had "accepted" as "collateral" shook on the market, he had refused extension of the loans, and taken the whole. Had simply opened his hand and closed it on everything Hill had left. Beatrice had a small trust fund from her mother, that was all.

He had got revenge on the tribe of Hill, all right! He'd been told that Beatrice tried to kill herself, and was only prevented by a nurse. . . .

The rooms were delicately beautiful, in a way representing the spirit of the girl who had grown to womanhood in them. There were no overhead lights.

The lamps were in wall brackets. These brackets were of carved crystal, and from the lamp-rings hung festoons of glittering crystal. Prisms, pear drops, pendants.

Meller stared at the softly glittering beauty of the crystals. Then his ever ready stick came up again. He lashed hard at one of the brackets. A shower of broken crystal, like dew-drops in sunlight, flashed to the polished floor. He went to the next, and did the same. In a moment there wasn't a crystal bracket left, in either bedroom or sitting-room. And with each thrust of his stick he felt as though he were smashing, hurting Hill himself.

IN THE bedroom he came upon something that once more drew laughter from his snarling lips, at the same time angering him when he recalled the home his own boyhood had known.

Near the living-room door, set in onyx in the wall, were a dozen little switch-handles. They were tiny ebony plugs in a house phone system.

There was something for you, by heaven! A private telephone system for the house alone. An elevator in a private home; a complete telephone service in a private home. The old pirate had done well for himself, hadn't he?

He read the names etched in tiny copper plates under the bell plugs. Butler, garage, housekeeper, first guest room, second guest room, drawing-room, blue room, conservatory, Mrs. R. J. Hill, Mr. R. J. Hill——

Meller's cane raised to slash at the little switchboard, but slowly it lowered again. His snarling grin, like the grimace of a hyena over carrion that is all, all his, touched his red, sensual lips.

A bell for R. J. Hill, eh? When his daughter wanted to talk to her father she pulled that little ebony handle, and the old boy answered. Ring R. J. Hill.

W. T.—5

54

Well, Hill was in hell now. Quite poetical that sounded. Hill in hell. Too bad his daughter couldn't try to put through a call for the old man *now!* Just as, in her helplessness, she had called on her father when she found out what had happened to her father's fortune. Standing in Meller's office, staring at Meller with incredulous, stricken eyes.

"*Dad! Dad——*"

Yeah! Call for R. J. Hill, and see what good it would do you.

The idea tickled Meller's not-too-sensitive sense of humor. Call for R. J. Hill. Page R. J. Hill. He ought to be in that end pot of boiling oil, boy. Get his attention, if the devils will let him alone for a minute, and tell him Herb Meller is paging him. Meller, the man he despised in life, and who has beaten him now. Call for Hill, from Mr. Meller. Maybe the old guy would come from hell in answer.

Meller's grin spread. His pudgy hand went up to the little switchboard. He touched with a tentative finger the plug over the name of the eagle-beaked old man who had awed him in life, but whom he had beaten in death.

Then, decisively, he pulled the little plug down. It was just like an office switchboard; the same in principle, if built of more elaborate materials. He was familiar with its workings.

He heard a bell ring, very softly, from somewhere. Old R. J.'s apartment? Or in hell?

It pleased him to imagine that he heard a faint, gruff voice answering. The voice of the man who had overpowered bankers and frightened promoters by sheer savage force of character.

"Hello," he said into the little phone. "Is this you, Hill? Is this you, you old——"

Profanity streamed from his lips, words he hadn't thought of since he had been a

W. T.—6

slum kid with the slime of the gutters as his playground.

"How do you like the owner of your house, Hill? Tell me I'm a crook who only stays out of jail because of the technicalities of the law, will you? Call me a shyster promoter and a robber of widows and orphans, will you? Announce before a board of directors that no decent man of business would associate with me? All right, *now* what do you think of me?"

He snapped the little lever back into place. Call R. J. Hill! Ring him in hell, and console him with what Meller had done to his daughter!

With his cane twirling jauntily, Meller went to the suite's bathroom. As big as a full room. Silver fittings; more crystal wall brackets. A pink marble tub. And how did you like that, by heaven? Pink marble, eight feet long! To coddle the body of Hill's precious daughter—a body that would now go clad in basement bargain-counter cottons, and like it. Would Beatrice Hill pass this site when there was a twenty-story hotel on it, and dream of that pink tub—taken from her, along with everything else, by the man who had outsmarted old Hill in the end?

Meller lit a cigar and tossed the burnt match into the tub. He went back to the sitting-room, grinning at the little switchboard as he passed. Call R. J. Hill, eh?

The hall door had swung almost closed behind him when he entered Beatrice Hill's apartment. Just before he got to it, to go out, he stopped. He thought he had heard a step outside and below. A slow step. . . .

He shrugged, as it was not repeated. He must have imagined the sound. But it put him in mind of the way old R. J. had walked in the last few years of his life. His feet had gone bad on him. When he couldn't avoid walking, he had done it like a slow-motion picture. Slow, painful progress forward. Step by step

55

on aching old feet. He had walked that way when he forced Meller from his office. Slow step after slow step, with Meller retreating back from his flaming old eyes. . . .

Another step. On the bare marble staircase, it seemed to be. A slow, dragging step. Unless he was still imagining——

No, there it was a third time. Distinctly a step. And it *did* seem to ring familiar. For a moment Meller tried to tell himself that he couldn't place the familiarity. But he could, all right. The step sounded—precisely like the step of old Hill.

He stared back toward the switchboard, and a distinct feeling of chill touched his spine. He had summoned Hill. Had Hill—answered?

It was a crazy thought. He laughed aloud, and puffed at the cigar in his teeth. He was reaching for the knob when he heard the step again.

Slow, labored. On the staircase, all right. Just like Hill's painful crawl. . . .

Hell, it was the butler! That was all. The butler was coming up to see what had held him here so long. . . .

But he hadn't been up here long. Only a few minutes. And he had distinctly told the fellow to get out—not to bother him—that he'd find his own way around.

Well, then, the old man was coming up to investigate the crash of that mirror, or of the crystal brackets.

But he'd have been up here before now, if that were the case. Quite a while had elapsed since he had made a noise up here. Besides, the butler was an old fossil, just like Hill. He'd have used the elevator if he meant to come up—not have climbed those endless marble stairs. . . .

Meller began to sweat a little. All the time he had been standing there think-ing, he had been hearing the steps, slowly, laboriously ascending the stairs.

The butler, of course, he insisted to himself, wiping perspiration from his flabby face.

Thump, thump. A step at a time. A slow, painful crawl. God, it did sound like Hill!

Meller began to wish to heaven he had not pushed the phone switch over Hill's name. He wished he hadn't called those things into the phone. *Had* he heard a faint hello when he first lifted the receiver?

"I'm full of the jitters," he muttered aloud, listening to the slow, slow steps up the interminable marble staircase.

Listening to the steps. One step at a time, as if a feeble but determined body were hitching itself up a stair at a time and then resting.

"You out there," he called. "But-ler——"

He had called it loudly. Echoes rang in the gray and silver room. His voice must have carried to the person on the stairs.

But there was no answer. Only more of the slow, labored steps. Closer now. Very near the top. And the door he was facing, the door he was so near, was right at the head of those stairs.

"Hey—you—out there——"

It was almost a scream that came from Meller's lips. Mad or not, the thought that that might really be Hill, come in answer to the blasphemous call, was drowning him in horror. Those slow steps were so *exactly* like old Hill's.

Step. A rest. Step. A pause. Step, step. Heavily, wearily, but indomitably, as someone — *someone* — ascended the stairs outside.

"My God——"

It was a moan that came from Meller's stiff lips. His cigar lay smoking on the bare floor. Then he drew a deep breath. Why, he was really trembling! This was a hell of a note! Meller, many times a millionaire at forty-one, feared as few in Chicago were feared—trembling in a vacant room at the sound of steps!

"You out there! If you're the butler—say so!"

The steps paused—at the top of the stairs. And there was no answer.

Meller's last courage began seeping out of him. His fingers went up tremulously. He plucked at his shaking lips. The steps resumed, with infinite effort, infinite doggedness. They stopped right outside the door.

Was it the butler out there, or wasn't it?

But it was, of course! Oh, God, it had to be! A dead man obey a summons of the living? No, no! That wasn't possible. Even in a deepening sea of horror that made his heart pound till he could taste blood in his mouth, he *knew* that.

The door moved a very little. He wouldn't have noticed it if he hadn't been staring right at it with glaring eyeballs. It had been an inch or so open. Now it was two inches. Swinging open a very little. As if only a breath of pressure had been applied to it. Pressure such as no real hand, no flesh-and-blood hand, would exert. . . .

"I can't stand this!" Meller panted. "I'm being a fool——"

His hand went out. He clutched the knob of the door.

He knew it was the servant out there. Hell—who else could it be? There were only the two of them in that house. Only the two of them. . . .

The door moved a little against his hand. Moved, slyly, eerily—not as any normal person would have moved it. The butler, by God—deliberately trying to frighten him! *It had to be the butler!*

He flung the door open with a scream that echoed through the whole great house, flung the door open—and stood swaying there; stood swaying and stricken for a few seconds before he fell. . . .

IT WAS half an hour before the butler came up the stairs. He had been in the kitchen. He had thought for a moment he'd heard a scream. But it was not repeated, so he had paid no more attention. The walls of the old mansion were thick.

He screamed himself, now, as he got to the top of the stairs and saw the thing in the doorway of Miss Beatrice Hill's apartment. Screamed just once and cowered back.

The man who had called himself Meller lay there, and his face—his face——

The butler managed to get to the phone in the hall and call the police. Then he fainted, as if he had been a woman.

He had never before looked at the face of a man who had been frightened to death.

ℐatan's Palimpsest

By SEABURY QUINN

Weird was the doom and evil was the influence that emanated from that mosaic picture on the wall—a startling thrill-tale of Jules de Grandin, ghost-breaker extraordinary

IT WAS a merry though oddly assorted party Philip Classon entertained at Saint's Rest, his big house beside the Shrewsbury: a motion-picture star, a playwright quietly and industriously drinking himself to death, one or two bankers, a lawyer, several unattached ladies living comfortably on their dower or their alimony, Jules de Grandin and me. Dinner had been perfect, with turtle soup, filet of lemon sole in sauce bercy, Canada grouse and an assortment of wines which caused my little friend's blue eyes to sparkle with appreciation. Now, as he sat with Karen Kirsten on the big divan before the roaring fire of apple logs and sipped his Jérôme Napoléon from a lotus-bud shaped brandy sniffer, he was obviously at peace with all the world.

"Mais certainement, ma belle," I heard him tell the actress in an interval between the efforts of the duet at the piano to retail the nostalgic longings of the old cowhand from the Rio Grande, "it is indubitably a fact. Thoughts are things. We may not see or handle them, nor can we weigh them in a balance, but they have a certain substance of their own. They can penetrate, they can permeate the hardest matter, and like the rose-scent in Monsieur Moore's poem, they will cling to it when it is all but worn away by time or smashed by violence."

"Sure of that, are you, de Grandin?" our host asked quizzically as he leant across the sofa back and rested one hand on the little Frenchman's black-clad shoulder, the other on the actress' gleaming arm.

"As sure as one can be of anything—only fools are positive," de Grandin answered with a smile.

"You're certain?"

"Positive, parbleu!"

As the laughter died away Classon nodded toward the curtained doorway. "We've a chance to test Doctor de Grandin's theory," he announced. "There's something in the gunroom I'd like to show you and see what effect it has."

Amid murmurs of mystified conjecture he led the way across the wide hall lit by a pair of swinging boat-shaped lamps which gave that odd, pale light that comes only from burning olive oil, swept aside the heavy Turkish hangings at the door and motioned us to enter.

The "gunroom" was a relic of the days when New Jersey had no need of conservation laws for game, and the fowling-piece and rifle were as much a source of daily meat as were the meadow, the pig-sty and the poultry yard. An ancestor of Classon's who built ships when Yankee mariners dropped anchor in every port from Bombay to Southampton had built Saint's Rest as sturdily as he built his craft, and though slaves' quarters and summer kitchens had long been turned to modern usages, like the gunrooms they still retained their ancient designations.

It was a lovely place. There was a walnut table of Italian make surely not a year younger than the Fifteenth Cen-

58

tury, French rosewood chairs upholstered in brocade which must have been worth its measurement in gold, a lacquered Chinese cabinet dating from the days when the Son of Heaven bore the surname Han; across one wall was hung a lovely verdure tapestry from Sixteenth Century Flanders depicting decidedly naughty *al-fresco* goings-on with the same lack of restraint as that displayed by that amazing little mannikin in Brussels which every year decants champagne with utter unconventionality.

With a taper Classon lit two oil-dish lamps—the house was wired for electricity, but I'd seen nothing thus far but the light of lamps and candles—and directed our attention to a white-wood table

"Adonis, that pale, lovely boy."

59

like an altar which stood just within their zone of radiance. "This is it," he told us, and it seemed to me there was a sharp intake of breath, almost like a sigh of pain, as he made the brusk announcement.

Something like the tabernacle of a Catholic altar showed aureately in the lamplight. Two feet in height by eighteen inches wide, pointed like a Gothic arch, plain and unadorned with ornament as a siege gun's shell, its dull mat gold shone dimly in the mounting luminance cast by the gently swaying lamps. "What is it? Is it a——" the querying babble started, but Classon raised his hand.

"This is just the frame," he answered. "Look."

He pressed a hidden spring and twin doors sprang apart, revealing three pictures integrated into one, all worked in deft mosaic. On the inside of the left-hand door there ranged a group of dancing youths and maidens clad in the chiton of the classic Greeks as modified for use in Constantine's Byzantium. The other panel bore a group of creeping children, nude and chubby with the chubbiness so dearly loved by early artists, while in the center, deep-set between the back-flung doors, there stood a slender, pale ascetic figure with a clout of camel's hair about his loins, rough sandals on his feet and a cross-topped staff in his right hand. The ancient artist had worked cunningly, so cunningly that the tiny lines between the variegated-colored marble were finer than the minute crevices in Chinese crackle-wear, and no detail of the groups or portrait had been lost. The saint's blue eyes, wide, deep and extraordinarily sad, seemed to look into our own with a searching, deep intensity, as though to chide us for the worldliness that lay within our hearts and say: "Behold these dancing youths, these creeping, puling

babes; the babes grow into youth and maidenhood and have their hour of silly pleasure, then comes old age and death and dissolution. Vanity, vanity; all is vanity!"

"Well?" Classon asked when we had gazed upon the ikon for a long moment in silence. "What d'ye see?"

"A sacred picture."—"Beautiful!"— "Exquisite!"—"Sweet!"—"Divine!"— "Superb!"—"Swell!"

THE fatuous comments fluttered thick as snowflakes, phrased according to the speaker's wealth or paucity of diction.

"Yes, of course, but what d'ye *see?* What's the picture of?"

"A saint?" I hazarded when no one else seemed willing to express conjecture.

"That's what you all see?" asked Classon, and it seemed to me there was an eagerness about his question and an air of quick relief entirely unwarranted by the triviality of the entire business.

I was turning to examine the Chinese cabinet when de Grandin's hand upon my elbow brought me round.

"Observe her, if you will, Friend Trowbridge," he commanded, motioning toward Karen Kirsten with his eyes.

She had not replied to Classon's questions nor expressed opinion of the ikon's artistry, I realized, but I was unprepared for what I saw. She was standing looking at the triple picture, head thrown back, hands hanging limply open at her sides. The lamplight played across her, accentuating her unusual beauty in a way no cameraman had ever managed. Tall she was, almost six feet, and every line of her was long, but definitely feminine. Her hair, like silver-silken filaments, was smoothed and plaited in long braids about her head; her dazzling fairness was set off by a slim gown of apple-green baghera draped in Grecian fashion; there were bracelets of carved gold upon her arms and a strand of pearls about her throat, and I caught my breath in sudden wonder, for lustrous pearls and lucent skin almost exactly matched each other. Her ice-blue Nordic eyes habitually held the commanding look which is the heritage of Northern races, but now there was another, different look in them. The pupils seemed to spread until they stained the blue irides black; I could see fear stealing into them, stark, abysmal fear which radiated from a sickened heart and was mirrored in her eyes.

"All right, folks," Classon's brusk announcement broke the spell; "that's all there is. Let's go back and have another drink."

"But why did you insist we tell you what we saw, Phil?" asked Mrs. Durstin as we reassembled in the drawing-room. "It's just an ordinary lovely piece of mosaic, isn't it?"

Classon laughed shamefacedly. "Just a gag, Clara," he assured her. "Didn't you ever notice how the average person can be bullied out of sticking to the evidence of his own senses? Why, I've had people here who declared they saw all sorts of things—even swore they saw the figures move—when I kept asking 'em what they saw in those pictures. Seems as if this is a pretty level-headed crowd, though; I didn't have a bit of luck with you."

The evening passed with a surprizing variety of liquid refreshment, some passable singing, much ultra-modernistic dancing and a number of stories, some of which were funny and risqué, some merely ribald. By midnight I had managed to convince myself that the vision of Miss Kirsten's terror in the gunroom had been due to some illness which had stricken her—any doctor knows what changes indigestion-pangs can work in patients' faces—and dismissed the recollection from my mind.

But as we paused to say good-night beside the stairs, Miss Kirsten laid her hand upon my arm.

"You and Doctor de Grandin drove down from Harrisonville, didn't you, Doctor Trowbridge?" she asked, and again I saw that flicker of stark terror in her eyes.

"Yes," I answered.

"How long are you staying?"

"Only to breakfast, unfortunately. I should have liked the opportunity of talking more with you, but——"

"Won't you take me with you, please?" she broke in on my clumsy gallantry. "There isn't any train till noon tomorrow, and I've been going utterly mad in this house all day. I must get away as quickly as I can. I must—*I must!*"

"Why, certainly," I soothed. "Doctor de Grandin and I shall be pleased to have you with us on the homeward drive."

"Oh"—her long, slim, delicately articulated fingers closed upon my arm with a grip of surprizing strength—"thank you, Doctor!"

She made me the offer of a grateful, half-frightened smile, lit her candle from the lamp of hammered bronze which burned upon the table by the newel post, and turned to mount the stairs.

ARRAYED in violet-silk pajamas and mauve dressing-gown, de Grandin stood before the window of our bedroom, looking out upon the snow-flecked darkness of the winter night as if he sought to light it with something burning in his mind.

"What's the matter, old fellow?" I asked, smothering a yawn as I made for the bathroom, tooth-brush in hand.

"I wonder," he returned without taking his meditative gaze from the black square of the window, "I ponder, I cogitate; there is a black dog running through my brain."

"Eh?" I shot back. "A black——"

"Précisément. An exceedingly troublesome and active small black poodle, my friend. Why?"

"I don't think that I follow——"

"Ah bah, you are literal as a platter of boiled codfish! When I ask why, I mean why. Why, by example, does our friend Classon want to have the testimony of his guests that that ikon in his gunroom is but the pretty picture of some dancing children and some creeping babes who act as foils for an ascetic saint? Why is he relieved when they tell him what they see. Why——"

"Didn't you hear what he told Mrs. Durstin?" I broke in. "It's some silly sort of game he played; he wanted to see if he could bully us into thinking that we saw——"

"What he has seen, maybe?"

"What *he* saw? Why, what could he see that we couldn't?"

"That which Mademoiselle Kirsten saw, perhaps."

"See here," I dropped into the armchair by the fire and felt for my cigarcase, "all this mystery has me slowly going crazy. Classon didn't seem in any jocose mood when he asked us what we saw while looking at that picture. Indeed, it seemed to me that he was definitely frightened, and when we told him that we saw the picture of a saint he seemed relieved, yet a little disappointed, too.

"Then take Karen Kirsten. I can't understand her. She's more like Brunhilde than Griselda; I'd say she never was afraid of anything. Twelve hundred years ago women like her swung double-bladed axes and tugged twenty-foot oars beside their men, and spat back curses and defiance in the face of god and devil; yet if that woman wasn't absolutely mad with horror of some sort—if she isn't hag-ridden and almost wild to leave this house this very minute—I never saw terror in a human face. Have you any idea what it's all about?"

He turned from the window and tore the blue wrapping from a packet of "Marylands," selected one of the evil-smelling things with infinite care and set it alight. "Not an idea, my friend, merely a thought; one of those vague, elusive thoughts that fade like dewdrops in the sun when you seek to put them into words. But——" He shook his head impatiently, as though to clear his brain, then recommenced:

"You saw the composition of those pictures, how they are constructed of cleverly matched bits of colored stone. Very good. Between the little colored fragments are tiny, so small lines, *n'est-ce-pas?"*

"Of course, it's a mosaic——"

"Bien. It was only for a moment, for the fraction of the twinkling of an eye, but as I looked upon those pictures I thought the colored marbles ran together, separated, turned about one another like the bright glass of a kaleidoscope and formed a different pattern. It was over quickly, *parbleu,* so quickly that it could hardly have been said to have occurred, but——" He paused and puffed reflectively at his cigarette, letting twin rivulets of smoke trickle slowly from his nostrils.

"What was it that you saw?"

"Mordieu, that is what taunts me. I cannot say. So quickly it came, so fast it disappeared that I had not time to realize it. But I am certain that it was an evil, an obscene and wicked thing I saw, like a monkey dancing on a consecrated altar."

"But that's absurd."

"The line of demarkation that divides absurdity from horror is often very finely drawn, my friend." For a moment he stared straight before him, and his little round blue eyes seemed misted, as though, still open, they shut out vision while he racked his inner consciousness for an answer to the riddle. Abruptly: "Come, let us go and look at it," he bade. "It may be in the quiet of the empty room we shall be able to congeal and hold that fleeting metamorphosis which mocked me when we stood there with the others."

We tiptoed toward the stairs, but hardly had we gone ten feet when his hand upon my arm brought me to a halt. In the dim light cast by a single swinging oil lamp someone was coming from the floor below, someone who walked in silence and whose presence we should not have realized had it not been for the shadow cast across the stairhead.

"Back into this doorway if you please, my friend," de Grandin whispered, and as we shrank into the recess of the deep-set door Karen Kirsten glided up the stairs, paused a moment with one hand upon the baluster and threw back her head with up-turned eyes as though imploring mercy from kind Providence. She was tense as a drawn harp-string, and her face was set in lines of suffering, but the faint light seeping up the stair-well from behind her rippled through her golden hair and cast shadows on her brows which seemed to deepen the cerulean of her eyes. In her sleeveless, neckless nightrobe of white crêpe, with a slender hand laid humbly on her heaving bosom, it seemed to me she bore a likeness to the pictures of Saint Barbara.

"Ah, God!" she breathed in a high, quivering sigh. "God have pity!"

Filled with compassion I took a half-step toward her, but the sudden pressure of de Grandin's small hand on my elbow halted me.

"Observe," he breathed—"*le sang!*"

I felt a retching wave of sickness as he spoke. Across the bodice of her nightdress where her slender hand had rested, was a dark, rubescent stain.

FOR an endless moment we three, watched and watchers, stood in statue-like stillness; then with another sobbing sigh the woman turned and glided down the hall, her white, bare feet as soundless as a zephyr on the polished boards.

"Wh—what can have happened?" I faltered, but his only answer was to urge me toward the stairs.

The pale glow of a single lamp burning like a vigil light above the altar-table where the ikon stood shone through the gunroom as we entered. At a glance I saw the little doors were open and the triple picture on display, but before de Grandin's quickly indrawn breath had sounded I had also seen the thing that lay before the table on the floor.

It was—it had been—Wyndham Farraday, the dissolute young playwright, and a single glance assured us he was dead. His head lay back, and in the staring, sunken eyes, pinched nose, drooping jaw and idiotically half-protruding tongue we read the signs that to the practised eye are unmistakable. He lay upon his back with arms thrown out to right and left as though he had been crucified upon the hardwood floor, and from the left breast of his pajama jacket thrust the gilded cross-shaped handle of a slender dagger, a mediæval misericord, thin as a darning-needle, pointed as a bee-sting, designed to slip between the links of fine chain-mail and deal the death blow where a larger weapon would have failed. A little sluggish stream of blood had stained his jacket round the knife-wound. He was not handsome or majestic as he lay there with the chill of *rigor mortis* even then beginning to congeal his loose-hung lower jaw. Poets and romantic writers to the contrary, there is little dignity or beauty in raw death, as every soldier, doctor and embalmer knows. The majesty of death is largely artificial.

"Do you think she——" I began, but

de Grandin's sudden exclamation broke my words.

"*L'idole*—the picture, my friend—observe her, if you please!" he breathed.

I looked, then blinked my eyes in wondering disbelief. The little bits of colored marble which composed the triple picture seemed sliding past, around and *through* one another with a bewildering kaleidoscopic motion, losing their old pattern, making vague, unformed designs upon their golden background, then re-arranging themselves in new and terrifying groupings. It was hard—impossible —to say what scenes they formed, but I felt a wave of nausea sweeping over me, a physical sickness such as that I felt when as a young interne I had been assigned to duty at the city morgue and for the first time smelled the fulsome odor of decaying human flesh.

Then sanity returned. The lamp! It was swaying pendulum-like above the ikon. That was it; the changing light and shadow as the light swung back and forth had caused an optical illusion. I took the boat-shaped bowl of burnished copper in my hands and steadied it. When I looked again the pictures had resumed their lovely wont. The youths and maidens once again danced joyously upon the tender, blue-green grass against a background of fresh-budding willows; the chubby cooing infants rolled and sported on a flowering sward; the pale, ascetic saint looked out with admonition and reproach upon a world which wooed the pomps and pleasures of the carnal life.

"Oh thou empty-headed zany, thou species of an elephant, thou—oh, *le bon Dieu* give me patience with this witless one!" de Grandin fairly chattered, his round blue eyes ablaze with indignation, his small hands twitching to close round my throat.

"Why, what's the matter now?" I asked. "That swaying lamp obscured our vision; we'll need a steady light to see——"

"If kindly Providence will defend me from my well-intentioned friends, I think that I can guard against my enemies!" he broke in sharply, looking at me with a heaven-grant-me-fortitude expression. "In your attempt at helpfulness you have blocked the path of justice, human and divine. That swinging lamp was not set in motion by itself, *par consequent* it must have started swaying by some outside force. I would make bold to venture that some human hand had touched it in the recent past, for it was still in motion when we came here. Accordingly, there were unquestionably finger-prints upon it. Whose? *Hélas*, that we shall never know. You must needs stop the light from swinging because it made you see things which were not there to see—and left your great and ugly paw-prints on it in the process. Twenty expert tracers cannot now find the prints which were left there by the person who had touched that lamp a little while before. And that person, I damn think, was none other than the murderer of this poor one.

"Also, the distortion of this picture, as you call it, which you have attributed to the swaying of that lamp, may be the very crux of all this cursèd mystery. Why was Monsieur Classon anxious to have the testimony of his guests that this pretty picture was nothing but a pretty picture? Because, I think, he had seen it show another scene, *pardieu!* Why did la Kirsten show such signs of fear when she looked upon this seventy-times-damned ikon? Because she saw a something which was not good to see while the others saw but pretty figures! Why did Jules de Grandin have impressions of some sacrilegious scene when first he looked upon this piece of what seems

W. T.—2

innocent mosaic? Because I am attuned to superphysical appearances; I see deeper into such things than the ordinary man. Finally, why did you look sick, as if your dinner had most vilely disagreed with you, when you looked at this cursèd picture but a moment since? Because you, too, saw something dreadful taking shape. A moment more and we had captured it—but you must be helpful and dispel the atmosphere of evil which was gathering thick as fog.

"And now you ask me what's the matter! You should abase yourself. You should repent in sackcloth; you should walk barefoot through the snow; you should abstain from liquor for a week, *parbleu!*

"No matter," he put aside annoyance with true French practicality and turned toward the door. "This is now a matter for police investigation. Let us telephone the state constabulary."

"**T**HIS is positively the most uncanny business I've ever seen," Captain Chenevert of the State Police informed us.

De Grandin eyed him saturninely. "You are informing me, *mon capitaine?*"

"I certainly am. Look here: We've checked and double-checked that room for finger-prints, and what do we find? Nothing. Not a thing!"

"Nothing?"

"Well, practically. Or, rather, something worse. There are plain and unmistakable prints on the dagger handle, but they're Wyndham Farraday's. Now, that just doesn't make sense. Farraday might have stabbed himself through the heart, though this job's so neatly done it almost seems as if a surgeon did it; but if he did it himself one of two things would have followed the infliction of the wound. Either he'd have staggered forward and fallen in a heap, probably on

W. T.—3

DR. DE GRANDIN

his side, or he'd have collapsed at once; in which case he would either have fallen face-forward or dropped upon his back with his legs partly doubled under him. Possibly—though this usually happens in cases of shooting through the brain—he'd have been seized with a cadaveric spasm, all his muscles would have tightened into knots, and his fingers would have closed round the dagger-hilt in an almost unbreakable grip."

He paused and looked at Jules de Grandin questioningly. "Do you agree?"

"Perfectly, *mon capitaine;* you have exhausted the possibilities of the situation from a scientific standpoint."

"Then why in blazing hell was he lying so neatly spread out on the floor with his heels together like a soldier at attention and his arms flung out at right angles to his body?"

"Mightn't someone wearing gloves have stabbed him after he'd had the dagger in his hand?" I hazarded; but:

"Not a chance!" Chenevert smiled bleakly. "We've considered that, but if it had been done that way Farraday's finger-prints would have been practically

65

obliterated, or at least smudged to some extent. They're not; they're clean and clear as any I've ever seen. This thing's got me going nutty. The finger-prints say 'suicide' with a capital S; all collateral evidence points to murder. If such a thing weren't palpably absurd here, I'd say it looked like *hari-kari*—ritual suicide with the assistance of a second party, you know. I saw a case of it in Kobe some years ago. A man had disemboweled himself in the approved Japanese manner, but the friend who acted as his second had waited to compose his limbs so that he lay as peacefully as Wyndham Farraday, though he must have threshed around terribly during the death agony."

Suddenly I saw it all. Karen Kirsten's frenzy to get away, her terror when she entered the gunroom last night, the blood on her nightgown when we saw her in the upper hall! It had been a suicide pact, and the woman lost her courage at the last. "By George," I exclaimed, "Miss——"

The kick de Grandin gave me underneath the table nearly broke my tibia, but it had the desired effect. "Mistakes like that are easy to make in such cases," I ended lamely as Chenevert cast a questioning look at me.

"Friend Trowbridge has the right of it," de Grandin nodded. "There are many angles to this case, my captain; the trail is long and winding, and involved. Perhaps it would be well to lay the household under interdict."

"Eh? Inter——"

"Perfectly. Until the guilty party is arrested or the case marked permanently unsolved, every person in the building is suspect. People have a way of disappearing, my captain, once they leave the jurisdiction. While all of us are here you can put the finger on us at convenience. Once we are scattered——"

"I gotcha," Chenevert laughed. "You bet I'll put the clamp on, Doctor. Can't hold 'em here indefinitely, but I'll post a couple of the boys here with orders not to let anybody leave for thirty-six hours. We should know where we stand by that time. Meantime," he wound his muffler round his neck and buttoned up his short coat, "there's the body to dispose of and reports to be prepared. Call me at the barracks if anything comes up. I'll be over again sometime this afternoon."

"OH, THIS is terrible!" Karen Kirsten wailed when we told her the police had forbidden us to leave. "I have shopping to do in New York, and my lawyers to consult about a new contract. I have to take a plane for the Coast immediately!" Her blue eyes blazed and her long hands folded and unfolded as she strode across the floor with her characteristic long-limbed, effortless walk. "I can't—I won't be cooped up in this dreadful place another minute, I tell you!"

True to the traditions of her trade, she was working herself into a temperamental tantrum, but beneath de Grandin's level stare she calmed amazingly.

"It would be better if we told ourselves the truth without reservation of any sort, *Mademoiselle*," he spoke in a level, almost toneless voice. "We are your friends; moreover, our experience has taught us to give credence to many things which the ordinary man would brush aside as nonsense. Nevertheless, we cannot help you if you are not frank."

"Why shouldn't I be frank?" she blazed. "I've nothing to hide. I know nothing of this dreadful business."

"You did not know that Monsieur Farraday was dead until they told you?"

"Of course not!"

"Not even when you left your room at dead of night and crept mouse-quiet to the gunroom where he lay like one crucified before that so queer ikon?"

"What do you mean? I never left my room last night——".

"*Mademoiselle*," he interrupted harshly, "you are lying. It was Doctor Trowbridge and I who notified the police of Monsieur Farraday's death when we stumbled on his body in the gunroom. As we were about to leave our room we saw you coming up the stairs, we saw the agitation under which you labored, we saw the blood upon your *robe de nuit*. We have not spoken of this, *Mademoiselle*, for there are some things best left unsaid, for the present, at any rate; but if you persist in this pretense of ignorance—if you will not help us to help you"—he spread his hands and raised his shoulders, brows and elbows in a shrug —"*eh bien*, it is a crime to withhold information from the officers, *Mademoiselle*. You would not have us become criminals, surely?"

She went absolutely rigid. There had never been much natural color in her cheeks; now they were positively corpse-gray. And her eyes were terrible in their fixed stare.

"You mean you saw me come upstairs last night?" she whispered. Her words were so low that we could scarcely hear them, her voice flat, expressionless, almost mechanical.

"Perfectly, *Mademoiselle*." The ghost of a hard smile curved the lips beneath the trimly waxed wheat-blond mustache. Surrender showed in the sudden drooping of her shoulders, in the lines of weariness that suddenly etched themselves in her carefully-tended face.

"Very well," she answered in a voice dull with fatigue, "I was there; I saw him—found him huddled up before the altar where that dreadful picture stands. He seemed so young, so helpless, lying there like that. I composed his limbs"—

her blue eyes filled with tears and her firm chin quivered with unbidden sobs— "I stretched his arms out, too. It was a dreadful thing he'd done; it's terrible to kill yourself, and I thought that if I stretched his arms out like a cross it might help him plead for pardon——"

"That was the *only* reason you arranged him so, *Mademoiselle?*" Again the flicker of a disbelieving smile showed upon his mobile lips.

"Oh"—the woman turned on him, her eyes gone flat with fright—"you're dreadful, uncanny, devilish! No, if you must have the truth! I stretched his arms out like a cross because I was afraid. There's an old belief in Sweden that the dead ride hard, that suicides are lonely on their way through hell, and come back to the world to look for company; but if you lay a cross across their path, their way back to this world is barred. They can't come at you, then. We forget these things in practical America, but Death's not practical; it's as old and terrible as Odin's raven or the Storm Sisters; it brings back thoughts of olden days, so——"

"Precisely, *Mademoiselle*, one understands. Now tell us, if you please, what made you seek the gunroom in the first place?"

"Give me a cigarette," she begged, and he held his open case before her, then held his lighter forward. As she touched her cigarette tip to the fire she looked at him across the tiny flame that gleamed its echo fascinatingly in her brilliant eyes.

"I've had devils ever since I came here," she told us. Her voice was slurred and languorous, almost somnolent, yet strangely mechanical, as though an unseen hand played a gramophone on which her words had been recorded. "I don't know what it was; ordinarily I'm not subject to nerves, even when I'm tired, but something in the very atmosphere of this house seemed to frighten me. Perhaps it was the eery half-light the place has even in the day, maybe the lamplight, so different from the bright glow of electricity to which I'm used. At any rate, I had the creeps from the moment I crossed the threshold; everywhere I went I seemed to feel eyes, dozens of pairs of eyes—evil, wicked, calculating eyes—boring right into my brain from behind. I'd turn around a dozen times in the process of crossing the room to see if someone really were staring at me, but it was no use, the eyes were quicker. No matter how fast I'd turn they'd get around behind me, and keep staring—*leering*—at me from the back."

She ground the fire of her cigarette out against the bottom of an ash-tray. "Last year I visited a psycho-analyst in Hollywood, and he hypnotized me. I can remember how I fought against it just as I was going off to sleep. I kept shrieking to myself inside my brain: 'No, no; I won't give up my consciousness; I won't let this man inside my secret soul!' but by that time it had gone too far, and I fell asleep despite myself. That's how it was here. Someone—some *thing*—seemed trying to creep inside my brain; to steal my mind—no, not quite that, rather, to crowd it out. I could feel the force of impact of an alien presence trying steadily to get inside me, and just as I fought against the hypnotist, so I fought against this threat here at Saint's Rest. Only this time I was prepared; I was warned against the attack in time; I felt the subtle influence that probed and clawed and dug at my integrity. And I fought it—*Gud*, how I fought it!

"IT WAS through Wyndham Farraday that I met Mr. Classon. I'd known Wyndham out on the Coast when he was doing some writing for Cosmic Films, and looked him up when I came East. He told me of a friend of his who had this wonderful old house filled with the most astonishing old relics, and said the pride of the collection was a reliquary brought from Constantinople when the Crusaders under Baldwin sacked it in 1204.

"I love old things. I've spent a fortune on them for my house in Beverly, and the thought of something like this fascinated me. Wyndham wanted Mr. Classon to take me to the gunroom right away, but he put us off with first one excuse and then another. We didn't go in till he took the others to see it after dinner last night, and by that time I was almost frantic. I felt that if only I could get away from this awful place I'd have nothing more to ask.

"The moment Mr. Classon took us in to see the ikon I *knew*. There, I realized, was the spider that sat in the center of the dreadful web which was entangling me. A spider—ugh! Spiders suck their victims' blood, I'm told, and just so this —this *thing*—had been sucking at my soul and sanity. I looked at the horrible, lovely thing with the same feeling of repulsion I'd have felt while looking at some beautiful venomous reptile in its cage. Only this thing wasn't caged. It was loose, and nothing stood between it and me. Then, as I looked, the colored stones in the mosaics all seemed to melt and run together, and form a sort of toneless gray. It seemed as though there were dull, lead-colored mirrors in the golden frames, and as I looked in them other pictures seemed to form. The dancing youths and maidens seemed to age before my eyes till they were dreadful dotards and hags, the little babies seemed to swell and puff to monstrous parodies of human children. The saint ——" her voice trailed off and her eyes became lack-luster, dead as painted eyes in a wooden statue's painted face.

"Yes, *Mademoiselle?*" de Grandin prompted softly.

"I—don't—remember," she said softly. "It was something terrible, some dreadful transformation that shook me like a chill, but I can't describe it."

"One appreciates your difficulty," the little Frenchman murmured. "And then?"

"Like a voice in a dream I heard Mr. Classon telling us to go back to the drawing-room, and it seemed to awaken me from a sort of trance I'd fallen into. I drank more than I should last night, but if I could get drunk, I thought, I might be able to escape the memory of those frightful figures in the pictures. Finally, when we said good-night, I asked Doctor Trowbridge if I might ride up with you this morning.

"I couldn't sleep. The recollection of the things I'd seen—all the more terrifying because I couldn't recall them clearly—kept torturing me, and I made up my mind to go down to the gunroom and have another look at the reliquary."

A faint smile raised the drooping corners of her mouth, and she looked at us diffidently, as though she begged for understanding.

"When I was a little girl we had a picture-book that scared me dreadfully. It was the story of Strongheart and the Dragon, and I'd feel my breath all hot and sulfurous in my throat when I looked at some of the illustrations. But I kept going back to it. I'd creep into the library, take it down from its shelf and, beginning at the first page, slowly turn the pages back, leaf by leaf, till I came at last to the picture showing Strongheart grappling with the Monster. 'It won't frighten you so much this time, you're getting used to it,' I'd tell myself as I came nearer and nearer to the terrifying picture. But it always did. When at last

I'd turned the final leaf and saw the awful, scaly thing with protruding, fiery eyes and forked red tongue and clutching claws staring at me, I'd seem to suffocate again, and run shrieking from the library to hide my face in Mother's apron.

"It was like that last night. I knew I'd be frightened almost past endurance if I looked at the ikon again, but I couldn't resist the morbid urge to go downstairs. Finally I gave up the struggle and crept down, fighting with myself at every step, and losing the contest at each stride. I was fairly running when I reached the lower hall.

"A light was burning in the gunroom, and it must have been set going recently, for the lamp was still swaying like a pendulum when I entered. I started for the picture, but before I reached it my foot struck something, and when I looked down there was poor Wyndham lying dead before me. I tried to scream, but the breath seemed to stick in my throat. I just stood there trembling, and in my brain a thought kept pounding: 'The picture made him do it—the picture made him do it!' "

"You say you knew he did it. One does not doubt your intuition, but how were you certain it was suicide, *Mademoiselle?*"

"Because there was a smear of blood on the heel of his hand, as if it had spurted out when he drove the dagger through his heart. If someone else had stabbed him he'd have thrown his hand up to his heart or tried to pluck the dagger out; the blood would have been on his palm or on his fingers."

"*Bravo,* an excellent deduction. And then——"

"I wiped the blood off his poor hand and wiped my own hands on my nightdress, then composed his limbs and laid him like a cross to bar his wandering spirit if it came back seeking company,

Then I crept back upstairs without stopping even to extinguish the lamp."

An agony of entreaty was in her face, and she clasped her hands imploringly, not theatrically, but instinctively, as she begged: "Please, please believe me. I've told you nothing but the truth. You don't think that I murdered Wyndham, do you?"

"We believe you utterly, *Mademoiselle*," de Grandin answered. "But what the police would think is something else again. It would be better if we kept our counsel, we three, and said nothing till we have had time to think."

"**N**ow what?" I asked as we closed our interview with Karen Kirsten. "I think that I should like a word or several with Monsieur Classon," he replied. "His anxiety to test his guests' reactions to that *sacré* picture was founded on no idle whim, my friend; there is something much decidedly more than meets the naked eye in all this business of the monkey, or I am vastly more mistaken than I think. Yes, of course."

But Philip Classon was nowhere to be found. We sought him in the drawing-room, the library, the little combination office and retreat which he had made above the ancient carriage house. Finally, all other places failing, we ventured to the gunroom. The night before we had observed that only a heavy Turkish tapestry closed off the gunroom from the wide central hall. Now, as we put the drapery back, we found our passage barred by a heavy sliding door which had been drawn and locked.

"*Sang du diable!*" de Grandin muttered when neither repeated knockings nor calls could elicit a response; "this is more than merely strange! He cannot have gone out, the police will not permit that any leave the premises without a pass from Captain Chenevert; he is not

in any of the other rooms; *alors*, he is in there. But who would go into that devil-haunted place, and why does he persist in keeping silent? *Parbleu*, but I should like to tweak him by the nose."

"Perhaps he doesn't want to be disturbed," I ventured. "Events of the last twelve hours have been enough to make him worry. If——"

"If he does not answer our next summons I shall force the door;" the little Frenchman interrupted. "I do not trust that gunroom, me. No, it is an evil place, the very temple of the evil genius which has haunted Mademoiselle Kirsten since she came here. *Holà*, Monsieur Classon, are you within? We have important matters to discuss!"

Utter silence answered him and with a sigh of vexation he went to seek the trooper who stood guard at the front door.

The young state constable was diffident. His orders were to watch the house and see that no one left. Regulations forbade the injury of private property unless a crime had been committed.

"*Morbleu*, a crime will be committed, that of assault and battery, if you refuse us aid," the little Frenchman blazed. "Am I not in charge here in Captain Chenevert's absence? But certainly. Are not *Monsieur le Capitaine* and I close friends, boon companions? Indubitably. Have we not been drunk together? It is entirely so. Break in the door, *mon vieux;* I will shoulder full responsibility."

Whoever built that door had understood his business, for it was not until de Grandin had added his weight to the stalwart young trooper's that the lock gave way and the heavy oaken panels slid aside.

"Good heavens!" I exclaimed as the gunroom stood revealed.

"Well, I'll be damned!" the trooper swore.

SATAN'S PALIMPSEST

"Dieu de Dieu de Dieu de Dieu!" said Jules de Grandin.

No lamp was burning in the room, and the heavy, rep-bound curtains had been drawn across the windows to shut out the howling storm, but enough light filtered through to make large objects visible. Almost in the selfsame spot where Wyndham Farraday had stretched out cruciform in death something half leant, half knelt in the gloom, its outlines proclaiming it a man, but its attitude terrifyingly inhuman.

It was—or rather had been—Philip Classon, and he leant obliquely forward with half-bent knees and dangling hands that almost touched the floor, and head bent oddly sidewise, mouth partly opened to permit a quarter-inch of livid, blood-empurpled tongue to find escape between the teeth displayed by curled-back upper lip and limply hanging, flaccid lower jaw. A strand of knotted rope was round his neck, its upper end made fast to the bronze ringbolt which secured the hanging lamp. The rope had been too long and Classon too tall to permit conventional suicide. It had been necessary for him to lean, almost kneel, in order to secure sufficient downward drag to strangle himself. Any time within the first few seconds after dropping forward he could have saved himself by merely standing upright, but unconsciousness follows swiftly on compression of the great blood-vessels of the neck. . . . He was grotesque but placid. There had been no death agony.

D E GRANDIN and I were regaling ourselves with black coffee liberally flavored with araq when Captain Chenevert stormed in after battling fifteen miles of snow-blocked roads.

"Another one?" he shouted angrily. "In the same room—within twelve hours? God A'mighty, this thing's gettin' to be a habit!"

Functionaries filled the house with utter chaos the remainder of the day. Photographers and finger-print experts from the police barracks; a sheriff's deputy, not quite clear as to either functions, rights or duties, but officiously anxious to impress us and the cynically polite state troopers with his own importance; the coroner, who being also the neighborhood mortician was wrung between the necessity of appearing appropriately grave and the difficultly suppressed delight at acquiring two cases from the same house in a single day. Finally the coroner's physician, a superannuated quack whose knowledge of post-mortem phenomena of suicide was plainly inferior to the state policemen's expert training. But at last the grisly business finished, and Classon left his house feet-first upon a stretcher, his mortality concealed but not disguised beneath a not-too-fresh white sheet.

Dinner was a dismal rite, its only spot of color Karen Kirsten's golden hair and vivid, scarlet lips. No one strove for conversation, no one had much appetite for food, but when we went into the drawing-room for coffee and liqueurs the appetite for alcohol was something more than obvious. By nine o'clock the women were thick-tongued and maudlin, the men sunk in the utter taciturnity of saturnine intoxication.

Karen Kirsten left us early, pleading headache, and de Grandin and I followed her as quickly as we could. There was too much of the solemnity and none of the jollity of a wake about that dim-lit drawing-room.

"Y OU'VE some theory," I accused as we shut our bedroom door against the dismal crowd downstairs. "What is it?"

71

"This afternoon I have been reading in the library of our late host," de Grandin answered as he lit a cigarette, "and what I read may throw some light upon these self-destructions. Mademoiselle Kirsten furnished us the clue when she told us that accursèd picture came from Constantinople. You are familiar with the culture of Byzantium?"

"Only vaguely."

"One assumed as much. Very well: The Greeks of that old city were an evil lot. For the most part they conformed to Christianity only outwardly, and conformity with them was largely but an overlaying of the ancient cults with a thin veneer of outward faith. At heart they never lost their paganism, and paganism, my friend, is far from being the sweet, pretty thing our pastoral poets would depict it.

"Diana of the Ephesians, the All Mother, sometimes known as *Magna Mater*, was no prototype of the Blessèd Virgin; quite otherwise, I do assure you. There were dark mysteries in the groves of Aricia beside the lake men called the Mirror of Diana. Dionysos, who has been so celebrated by our neopagan poets that we commonly regard him as a hearty boon companion, was far from being so. True, he, was the god of women, wine and song, but his women were harlots, his wine was drunkenness, his songs the ditties of the brothel. At his midnight festivals men and women cast their garments off and ran with staring eyes and unbound hair between the swaying trees, frenzied with the worship of their god, and his worship was unbridled lust. Little children were caught up by grown men and women, oftentimes their own parents, and forcibly initiated in the rites of drunkenness and carnal love. Aphrodite's priestesses were mere strumpets, working openly in competition with the common women of the town. Adonis, that pale

lovely boy so famed in poetry and picture, was worshipped with the sacrifice of boars. *Ha*, but there were places where his female votaries, anxious to assimilate their god through the intervention of his sacred animals, assumed the name and rôle of sows!

"Such were the deities of paganism. They were not gods, but devils. Yet for hundreds of years they had been worshipped with revolting ceremonies. Would people long accustomed to a religion of drunkenness and lechery willingly forgo it for the gentle, simple rites of Christianity? Not willingly, but Constantine the great gave them their choice of Cross or sword, and they chose the Cross. Yet ever the old and wicked faith persisted, always there were found some worshippers of the old ones in the secret places.

"*Bien.* It was not safe to flaunt their heathen practises. The lictors of the Emperor were ever on the watch for those who frequented suspicious gatherings; so, like the gambling-houses in your puritanical communities where gaming is prohibited, they must perforce resort to subterfuge. They had chapels to all outward seeming dedicated to the holy saints, and in those chapels they had furniture which semed devoted to the Christian worship. But as the witty Monsieur Gilbert says in his opera *Pinafore*, 'Things are seldom what they seem.' A quick change here, the drawing of a curtain or pressing of a hidden spring there, and the sacred Christian ikons become horrid instruments of evil, base scenes which pander to the passions like those which graced the obscene sanctuary of the goddess Aphrodite.

"But in some instances these Christians-who-were-no-Christians did not depend on anything so crude as mere mechanical appliances. They had skilled workmen make the holy images, sacred pictures, sacerdotal vessels which by means of cunning spells and conjurations were endowed with power to change their aspect of their own accord when the concentrated thought of evil persons focused on them. Happily, we do not know just what these wicked old ones' magic was; we do know that it comprehended human sacrifice and defilement of the sacred things of Christianity. We know also that periodically it was necessary that a victim be immolated, else the evil power of these Jekyll-Hyde things made of gold and stone and silver would be lost.

"Now, Friend Trowbridge, thoughts are things. Who is it that is not unpleasantly impressed when standing in a dungeon of the bad old Middle Ages? Who can look upon the blade of that blood-thirsty guillotine with which so many brave and lovely necks were severed while the Terror raged in *la belle France* and forbear to shiver? Who can hold a hangman's rope within his hands and not have feelings of a vague uneasiness? No one but the veriest clod, *pardieu!* For why? Because, I tell you, thoughts are things. The evil passions, the emotions of hatred, anger or despair which flowed so freely round these solid objects soaked into them as water penetrates a porous stone. And ever and anon those very thoughts are loosed—exhaled, if you prefer the term—upon the world again.

"*Bien. Très bien. Tout va bien.* In Monsieur Classon's books I read something of the history of this so hateful picture which he showed us. The Crusaders under Baldwin stole it from a Christian chapel when they sacked Constantinople. *Ha,* but the one who brought it back to Venice soon discovered his mistake! He set it up upon the altar of a church, and straightway evil things began to happen. Good women

DR. TROWBRIDGE.

praying at that altar turned to strumpets; mild, godly men were roused to deeds of lust and violence. At last the good priests exorcised the lovely, evil thing; then to make assurance doubly sure, got rid of it.

"But Italians were Italians then as now. Instead of throwing it away, destroying it, they sold it to a Frenchman! "Piously, my guileless countryman took the vile thing home with him and made an offering of it to a house of Benedictines. *Nom d'un rat,* within a month all hell had broken loose in that community! The monks forgot their vows, and I regret to state the nuns did likewise. They mortified the flesh with mutton pie on Fridays, they drank sweet wines and sang some tunes which had a most unchurchly air, and other things they did which more befitted soldiers and women of the camp than sober-lifed conventuals. It was a gay and naughty time they had until the bishop heard of it.

"CAME the Revolution. Tired of being trodden underfoot the people rose, and like a rabid, sightless beast struck right and left in frenzy, cutting down the just and unjust in their anger. The convents and religious houses were suppressed and sacred vessels melted down and turned to money to assist the Government in waging war against the foreign despots who would seat a king again upon the throne of France and place the tyrant's heel once more upon the people's neck. But not this one, *hélas!*

"An English milord bought it and took it to his *triste* and foggy little island. *Eh bien,* he was quite a fellow, that one! The things he did were shocking, even to a generation which was noted for its tolerance. If he coveted a neighbor's wife that neighbor would have been advised to say his paternosters, for our gallant lord was skilled in sword-play and could crack a wine-glass stem at twenty paces with his pistol bullet. Also it appeared that Satan was a loving guardian of his own; for when the injured gentleman sent friends to wait on the seducer of his wife or fiancée or daughter, he might have saved his heirs much trouble if he had sent messengers to interview the clerk, the parson and the sexton, for he soon had need of all their offices.

"*Tiens,* the devil is a mocker, always. After many years of startlingly successful sin our noble lord was caught red-handed as a card cheat. His fortune had been wasted by extravagance, the Jews of Lombard Street refused to lend him further money on his lands, he became a bankrupt and perished miserably in debtor's prison.

"Among the items seized by creditors was this same accursèd picture. For years it gathered dust in storage, then was put on sale at auction. Monsieur Classon's uncle purchased it, but luckily for him he kept it in a safe deposit box, and not until a year ago was it brought out and placed among the treasures of the gun-

room. Again his luck held good, for he was much away from home, and though there were some stories of some naughty intrigues in the servants' quarters, who knows if these were influenced by the presence of the picture in this house or simply the result of poor, weak human nature?

"At any rate *Monsieur* the Senior Classon died and his nephew took possession of this house and all things in it. When did he first perceive this picture of the saint was not as other pictures? One wonders. Surely, he must have noticed it, for it had him greatly worried. A Frenchman, an Italian, an Irishman or Highland Scot, even a Spaniard, perhaps, would at once have recognized that there was something *outré,* other-worldly, in the way that picture seemed to change its scenes and in the feeling of repulsion yet attraction it engendered in him. But certainly. These people have imagination. But Americans and Englishmen? *Non!* 'This thing is not in keeping with the general rule of things,' they would tell themselves. 'Me, I have seen things, things which most certainly are not there to be seen. Therefore it is my eyes which are at fault. I shall consult an oculist. I have felt things I never felt before; I have felt the power of utter, concentrated wickedness. I am not like that, me. No, I go to church five Sundays in the year, and pay my taxes and obey such laws as it is convenient to obey. I am a thoroughly good citizen, an Anglo-Saxon; I do not believe in fairies, Santa Claus or witchcraft, even if I do put credence in the literature that stock-promoters send me. This feeling of malaise I have whenever I am near that picture is due to indigestion. *Voilà,* I shall buy some pills next time I pass a pharmacy.' Yes, my friend, that is the way of it.

"But Monsieur Classon was not easy in his mind. He had seen things, he had felt things that neither spectacles nor patent medicines could cure. And so instead of seeking someone competent to give advice, he tried experiments upon his friends, asked them to the gunroom, bade them look upon this old Greek ikon and tell him what it was they saw. If they saw nothing strange he took their testimony as evidence that his feelings of discomfort and his visions of unpleasant things had come from his disordered faculties, not from some outside source. *Tiens,* that way madness lay."

"But granting all you say, and it seems incredible, what induced Farraday to stab himself?" I asked.

He teased the needle-points of his mustache between a thoughtful thumb and forefinger. At length:

"Ecstasy is hard to reason with," he answered slowly. "We see it manifest itself in various phases. The nun who kneels in breathless adoration at the altar feels no discomfort though the cold stones bite her knees till the flesh is almost separated from the bone. The Indian fakir and the Moslem dervish inflict unutterable tortures on themselves, yet feel no pain. Devotees of olden gods, Aphrodite, Moloch, Dionysos, Adonis, cut and hacked and cruelly mutilated their bodies while ecstatic fervor gripped them. Monsieur Farraday was a highly nervous, highly imaginative, highly organized man. Influences which would not affect the average person took tremendous hold on him. He had lived not long, but much. It is probable there was no sensation which he had not tasted sometime. The lure to self-destruction grows more potent as we deplete the possibility of fresh experience. That the evil influence of this picture swayed him we can hardly doubt. He had hidden it, but he induced Mademoiselle Kirsten to come and see it. Why? Merely because it was an ancient thing of lovely workmanship? I cannot think so. Deliberately, having felt the lure and terror and excitement which inevitably followed a period of gazing at that evil picture, he desired to initiate her into them. It was like the drug addict who seeks to corrupt others to his evil practises. Yes, that is so."

"And Classon?"

"We cannot surely know. He has sealed his lips; but I think if he could talk he would tell a tale of slowly mounting terror, yet a fascination which would not let him leave off looking at the dreadful scenes he saw when the picture changed its aspect. Like Mademoiselle Kirsten and the book which terrified her so, he must needs go back and back to look and look again upon that which no human eye should see. It was like a siren-song luring him to sure destruction. When his friend Farraday had broken with the strain and sacrificed himself a votive offering to sin, the strain on Monsieur Classon was past bearing. Perhaps his reason snapped, perhaps he felt an impulse to emulate his friend—any police officer knows that suicidal impulses are contagious. *En tout cas,* there it is. Farraday is dead, self-murdered, Classon is dead by his own hand——"

"And Miss Kirsten?" I broke in.

"*Précisément,* Mademoiselle Kirsten. I think we shall do well to watch that lovely one, both for her sake and ours."

"Ours?"

"Perfectly. If we keep close watch on her we shall prevent her emulation of those other poor ones; also we may find that she will guide us to an explanation of this Christian-heathen ikon."

"But good heavens, man! We've been chatting here for hours; she may have gone and——"

"No fear," he interrupted with a smile. "Me, I took the care. The gunroom door I nailed tight shut, for I was certain if she meant to harm herself it would be on the same spot where the others offered up their lives, and—*mordieu*—*nom de nom de nom de nom!* Why had I not thought of it before?"

"What in the world——"

"*S-s-sh*, my friend, keep still; be silent as the *chauve-souris* when she goes flitter-flitting in the twilight. Me, I have the inspiration, the idea, the—what you call him?—hunch. Yes."

He tiptoed down the corridor till he stood outside Miss Kirsten's door, then, almost in a shout, announced, "Yes, my friend, it is amazing. I cannot think how I forgot it. The gunroom door is nailed tight shut, but the windows are unfastened. I must have them nailed the first thing in the morning."

Making more noise than the occasion semed to warrant, he tramped back to our door and slammed it, shoved me unceremoniously aside and seized his woolen muffler from the dresser.

"Come," he commanded as he wound the reefer round his neck, "I do not think we shall have long to wait."

"What the dickens are you up to?" I demanded as he led me down the stairs, taking care to step on the innermost edges of the treads so that no telltale squeak should give warning of our descent.

"Cannot you see? I have given her the hint, shown her how the way is open. If she feels the mastering-urge to seek the gunroom, perhaps intent on suicide, she will surely do it now, and through the open window. We must be there first."

I T WAS cold and quiet as a mausoleum in the empty gunroom as we clambered through the window. In accordance with custom a fire had been laid on the andirons, but no logs had burned there since the night before, and the eery chill which permeates all empty places filled the darkened chamber to its farthest corner. Stabbing through the darkness with his flashlight, de Grandin finally decided on the space behind a yellow-taffeta upholstered sofa as the spot to lay our ambush, and we sank down to begin our vigil.

I had no way of telling time, for de Grandin had insisted that we leave our watches off lest their ticking warn our quarry of our presence. My feet grew cold, then stiff, then "full of pins and needles" as I crouched behind the couch. We dared not talk, we hardly dared to change position lest the creaking of a board betray us. At last, when I was willing to affirm on oath our vigil had endured a month, I felt the pressure of de Grandin's fingers on my elbow. Slowly, soundlessly, but steadily, the window opposite to where we crouched was being raised. In the half-light shining from the snow outside we descried a figure almost shapeless in the gloom, but plainly feminine.

The rasping of a match, the little flare of orange flame against Egyptian darkness, the pale, clear glow of burning olive oil as the hanging lamps were lighted, showed us Karen Kirsten.

She had thrust her bare feet into fur-lined carriage boots, and with one hand she held her coat of priceless sable tight across her breast. Her eyes shone phosphorescent in the lamplight's glow, like the eyes of an animal. Her lips' moist crimson and the pearl-hard sheen of little teeth between them fascinated me. Unbidden came the thought of Clarimonde, of Margarita Hauffe and her victims.

She faced the ikon and we saw her bosom heave beneath its sheath of gleaming fur. Her breath came rasping, grindingly, almost like the labored breathing of a patient *in extremis* with nephritis. A little skirl of laughter stung her scarlet mouth, not loud, but terribly intense. I thought that never had I heard a cry more blasphemous than that light cachinnation.

Her eyes were straining toward the ikon which she had thrown open so its triple picture caught the full force of the ever-shifting beams which slanted downward from the swinging lamps. They were fixed, intense, half closed, as though the violence of her gaze was too annihilating to be loosed direct; it seemed as though the very substance of her soul and body would pour out of those set, staring eyes.

"Master," came her thin-edged whisper, mordant as a storm-blast in December, "lord, possessor, ever-living conqueror of flesh and soul and spirit—I am here!"

She kicked the fur-topped boots from off her feet and put her hands up to the collar of her coat, throwing back the garment and permitting it to fall in coruscating brown-black coils upon the floor behind her. Then with a wrench she tore her marigold-hued negligée from throat to hem.

Whiter than a figure carved from Parian marble, whiter than an image fresh-cut from new ivory she stood before the altar-table with its golden-gleaming ikon in her pallid slenderness.

It was no wonder that two hundred million movie-fans were mad about her, for she was beautiful almost past describing. Her graciously turned arms, her slender, gently swelling hips, her tapering legs, her full, high, pointed breasts were utterly breath-taking in their loveliness. The Greeks had a word for her, *chryselephantinos*—formed of gold and ivory!

Strangely mystic she stood there; more mysterious, the odd thought came to me, in the starkness of her nudity

than when hidden in the swathe of clinging garments.

Statue-still she stood, only her left hand moving a little as it fluttered upward toward her breast, then forward, like a tower toppling when its cornerstone is wrenched away, like a silver-birch tree crashing when the axman's final stroke cuts through its roots, she fell face-downward on the floor and lay there motionless.

The lamplight glimmered on the whiteness of her body and the bright gold of her hair, flecking, flowing shadows interchanging quickly with bright spots of light as she clasped her hands behind her neck and beat her forehead softly on the floor before the ikon.

"The pictures—*mort d'un rat!*—see the pictures, good Friend Trowbridge; do you see them now?" de Grandin whispered in my ear.

I saw, and a wave of retching nausea swept across me as I looked.

How it happened I know not, but the little bits of colored stone which formed the pictures in the ikon had rearranged themselves, leaving the compositions of the scenes unchanged, but the subject-matter utterly transformed. Where the group of laughing youths and maidens had been dancing there was now a ring of naked, scrawny parodies of men and women holding hands and dancing back to back in the dreadful rigadoon which marked the witches' sabbat. Where the pretty babes had crept in infantile delight was now a crowd of edematous, hideously bloated monsters, obscenely tumefied, their faces formless as the features of a creature molded out of dough, yet with enough resemblance to the human countenance to show the nightmare grins which stretched their livid mouths and creased their puffy cheeks. They crept and crawled and sprawled upon each other like sightless slugs which

77

come to light when rotting logs are lifted, nor could I say if they were filled with loathing or obscene affection for each other as they intermingled all but formless bodies in a sort of fictive struggle.

But the center panel showed the greatest metamorphosis of all. The saint had shed his penitential garment of rough camel's hair and in its place his loins were girded with a leopardskin. The cross-topped staff was now a spear with gleaming lance-head; rawhide clogs had turned to golden buskins laced up the leg with straps of scarlet leather; a wreath of wild wood-roses bound his hair. It was a figure of sheer beauty, slender, straight, white-limbed and white-bodied as a girl, with a face too delicate to be a man's, not soft enough to be a woman's. The stern, forbidding glance had vanished, yet the eyes had lost no whit of their compulsion. They seemed to catch and hold all other eyes, they burned and smoldered with an intolerable sadness, yet their brightness was so great that it was fairly dazzling.

"*Mon Dieu*, it is the Lord of Evil!" Jules de Grandin whispered. "Satanas, Lucifer, Adonis!"

A CHILL we had not felt before came through the room. It was not the hard bitterness of the storm wind thrusting through the partly opened window, nor the close, still cold of a place long empty and unheated; there was an otherworldliness to it, the utter gelidness of the freezing eternities of interstellar space, a cold which seemed to paralyze the soul and spirit even as it numbed the body. Perhaps it was a trick of shifting lights caused by the swaying of the swinging lamps, but I could swear that on the wall behind the altar where the ikon stood there formed a patch of gloom, a shadow-shape which etched a figure in dull silhouette. And it was a figure of fear. Bat-winged it was, and horribly malformed, with slanting brow, protruding chin and great tusks jutting upward toward a nose which had the outline of a predatory vulture-beak. Great claw-armed hands attached to scaly arms seemed reaching outward through the semi-dark to fasten on the woman prostrate on the floor.

"*Attendez-moi*, my friend," de Grandin whispered; "do exactly as I say, or we shall lose our lives, perhaps our souls as well. When I step forward, do you take up anything that comes to hand and with it strike that cursèd ikon from its place. When you have struck, strike on, and keep on striking till you have demolished it completely. Oh, do not stop to bandy silly questions, friend; three lives depend upon your doing as I say, believe it!"

Mystified, but willing to obey his orders, I nodded mute assent, and reached up for a double-bladed Tartar ax which hung clamped to the wall above us.

"*Monsieur*"—de Grandin stepped from his concealment and bent his body stiffly from the hips as though addressing someone formally—"*Monsieur le Démon*, we will fight you for her. We are but mortal men, but by the faith we hold and by the strength that faith imparts, we fling our gage into your face, and offer you wager of battle for this woman's soul and body. More, if that is not enough, we will pledge our own, as well!"

It was not quite a laugh that answered him, indeed, it was not any sound which human ears can record; rather, it was as if a feeling, a subjective impression, of boundless and colossal scorn swept through the room, and like a dried leaf borne before the wind the little Frenchman was hurled back against the wall with an impact so terrific that I heard his bones crack as he struck the plaster-covered brick.

"Remember my instructions, good Friend Trowbridge—*strike!*" he gasped while he strove to wrench himself from the position into which he had been forcd by that unseen malevolence.

He was suffering, I could see. The force with which he struck the wall had knocked the breath out of him, and something which I could not see was pressing on his throat, his diaphragm, his limbs, and held him with his arms outstretched and head thrown back as though he had been crucified. He gasped and fought for breath, but the struggle was uneven. In a moment he would fall unconscious from asphyxia, for no air could reach his lungs, and his lips were even then beginning to show blue while his eyeballs started from their sockets.

Across the room I leapt, swinging my double-bladed ax about my head and bringing it down with all my might upon the golden ikon on the altar.

It seemed for an instant that I had cut into an electric cable, for a shock of numbing pain ran up my forearms, and I all but dropped my weapon as I staggered back.

"*Bravo, bravissimo,* my friend; that was nobly done!" De Grandin's voice was stronger, now; he had managed to inhale a breath of air, but even as he cheered me came a rattling in his throat. He was being throttled by his unseen adversary.

I struck again, and this time swept the ikon to the floor. It fell face-downward, its pictures hidden from my sight.

A surge of sudden wild, insensate anger swept through me. How or why I did not know, but this picture somehow was responsible for Jules de Grandin's plight. When I assaulted it he gained a temporary respite, in the momentary

pause between my blows he suffered strangulation. I went stark, raving mad. For a wild, exhilarated moment I knew the fury and the joy our Saxon forebears felt when they went berserker and, armor cast aside, leapt bare-breasted into battle.

I felt my ax-blade cleave the ikon's golden plates, wrenched it free and struck again; chopping, hewing, battering. The heavy golden plates were bent and broken, now, and little bits of colored stone were strewn about the floor where my furious assault had smashed the priceless mosaics. I drove my ax-head through the center panel, cleft the figure of the beautiful young man in twain, cut the dancing horrors into bits, smashed the crawling infantile monstrosities to utter formlessness; finally, insane with murderous rage, drove the battered golden casque into the fireplace as a hockey-player might shoot the puck into the goal-net, then reached up frenziedly, dragged down a hanging lamp and dashed it on the logs which lay in order ready for the match.

The dry wood kindled like a torch, and as the leaping ocherous flame licked hungrily at the shapeless mass which had a moment earlier been a priceless relic of the tessellater's art, de Grandin staggered forward, gasping thirstily for air like a diver coming to the surface after long immersion.

"Oh, excellent Friend Trowbridge, *brave camarade; camarade brave comme l'epée qu'il porte, parbleu,* but I do love you!" he exclaimed, and before I could defend myself had flung his arms around me, drawn me to him and planted a resounding kiss upon each cheek.

"I'm sorry that I lost my head and wrecked that lovely thing," I muttered, gazing ruefullly at the melting gold and flame-discolored fragments of bright marble in the fireplace.

"Sorry? *Mort de ma vie*, it is your sober reason that speaks now—and when has truth been found in staid sobriety? Your instinct was truer when it urged that you consign this loathsome thing to cleansing fire. *Tiens*, had someone had the wit to do it seven hundred years ago, how much misery would have been averted! *Pah*" —he seized the poker and probed viciously at the remnants of the reliquary — "burn, curse you! Your makers and your votaries have stewed and fried in hell for centuries; go thou to join them, naughty thing!" Abruptly: "Come, we have work to do, Friend Trowbridge; let us be about it."

We draped the sable coat round Karen Kirsten, drew the fur-trimmed boots upon her feet, bundled up her tattered negligée, then, quietly as a pair of burglars, took her through the window, through the service-pantry door, and upstairs to her bedroom.

"It is well *Monsieur le Capitaine* had but two men set to watch the house," de Grandin chuckled as we got the girl's pajamas on and drew the bedclothes over her. "The young man who snores so watchfully before the kitchen door would be surprized if he could know with what impunity his charges come and go at will, I think."

"I SUPPOSE you're going to tell me thoughts are things, and that explains the goings-on we've witnessed?" I accused as we got into bed.

"By damn, I am," he answered with a sleepy laugh. "If it were not so I should have had a merry chase to find a reason for these evil doings. Attend me, if you please: That ikon might be called a devil's palimpsest. First the olden, wicked tessellaters contrived the scenes we saw tonight, the wicked worshippers of evil gods who danced together back to back, as in the days when dancing wid-

dershins paid honor to the pig-faced Moloch, the terrible, amorphous things which typified primeval wickedness, finally the Lord Adonis. Then by a trick of cunning workmanship they overlaid their true design with those sweet, innocuous scenes of innocence, and in the center set the picture of a saint. 'Beauty is in the beholder's eye,' the ancient proverb says. It might have added that wickedness and goodness are to a great extent the same. Only when summoned by deliberate thought of evil did the underlying pictures dedicated to the unclean worship of the evil old ones come to light; at other times the ikon showed an air of innocence. *Ha*, but that was in the very long ago, my friend. Like a jar of porous earthenware filled constantly with aromatic liquids, this ikon was the center of a very evil worship, the receptacle of concentrated thoughts of wickedness and hate. Thoughts are things; they filled the very substance of the ikon as the aromatic liquors will in time so permeate the fiber of the earthen jug that it will always afterward give off their scent. Yes, certainly.

"In time the evil principle became so strongly concentrated in this ikon that it changed unbidden from its good to wicked aspect, and this was so especially when the person who beheld it harbored secret thoughts of sin. More, it added to, it strengthened these desires for evil. Did the person in its presence have suppressed longings to forsake the ways of soberness and take to drink? His resolution to remain a sober citizen was straightway weakened to the breaking-point, his thirst for drink increased tenfold. And so right through the Decalogue. Whatever secret evil one had struggled with and conquered became so magnified when he came in this ikon's presence that he was unable to resist the sinful urge. He was vanquished, beaten, routed, lost in sin.

W. T.—3

80

"And as person after person yielded to its wicked influence this devil's tool waxed ever greater in its strength. Eventually it was not necessary for the one corrupted to have harbored evil thought; he need only be impressionable, psychic, to behold the changing of the pictures and, unless he had unusual strength of character, to succumb to their foul lure. Karen Kirsten realized this when first she stepped into the gunroom; Wyndham Farraday had suffered from the same experience; often Philippe Classon must have seen those pictures change; it was that which preyed upon his mind and made him seek to lull his fears by having others look at them and hear the testimony which they gave. You see? It is quite simple. Yes. Thoughts most assuredly are things."

"But why should they select Adonis as typifying Evil?" I demanded. "As I recall it, he was a shy young man whom Venus wooed——"

"In Monsieur Shakespeare's poems, yes," he interrupted, "but not in the belief of those who worshipped Evil for its evil self. No, not at all; by no means.

"When those wicked ones were gathered to make mock of holy things and bend the knee to sinfulness, they invoked some god or goddess of the ancient days, or, in later times, the devil. At gatherings of devil-worshippers it was not always as a hairy man or goat that the devil was adored. He had other aspects, too. Sometimes he came as a most beautiful young man, Lucifer the Light-bearer; as Baron Satanas, cold, haughty, proud, but most distinguished in appearance; sometimes as Adonis, the young man beautiful and cold as ice, impervious alike to little children's lisping pleas or woman's charming beauty—it was not bashfulness, but utter, cold indifference that made Adonis proof against the blandishments of the Queen of Love and
W. T.—4

Beauty. He it was—still is, *parbleu!*—who gave nothing in return for worship but lies and bitter disappointments.

"Besides, the men who made those pictures and the worshippers who bent the knee before it were Greeks; degenerate Greeks, of course, but still inheritors of the culture that was Athens. A Greek could not do homage to a god, even to a god of evil, who was anything but beautiful."

"That dreadful shadow that we saw, the shadow that seemed to detach itself from the wall and reach toward Karen Kirsten just before you challenged it?" I asked. "That was——"

"Thought made manifest, my friend. The evil thought which for generation upon generation had been poured upon that cursèd ikon, that devil's palimpsest. It was the same thought that induced rebellion in the heavens against the power of good, the thought which prompted Cain to slay his brother, which brought the sacrificial babes to Moloch; *parbleu,* it was everything that is detestable and vile concresced into that little reservoir which was that never-to-be-sufficiently-anathematized palimpsest of Satan!"

"IT's positively the damndest thing I ever saw," swore Captain Chenevert next day. "Two killings in that room with no more clues to 'em than if they'd been in China. Then someone sneaks in there last night and smashes up a piece of bric-à-brac so valuable that no one can appraise it. Hanged if it doesn't almost seem as if the place were haunted!"

"I damn think you have right, *Monsieur le Capitaine,*" de Grandin answered, his face expressionless as a death mask.

He reached out for the bell-pull: "Will you have Scots or Irish with your soda water, gentlemen?"

The Withered Heart

By G. G. PENDARVES

*A strange story about the evil heart of Count Dul, which continued to
pulsate for two hundred years after its owner's death—a tale
of the dire catastrophe that took place when the
Count's half-forgotten grave was opened*

DEAR JOHN,

*If a fifteen years' friendship
means anything to you, come at
once. Sorry to hustle you like this, good
old slow-worm that you are, but we've simply got to go into session about this thing
before the month's out. The Ides of March
are on Tuesday next, May 31st, this year.
My whole future is at stake and you've
got to come and help. It's a very very
queer thing, and Jonquil and I don't agree
at all about it. I wish to heaven we'd
found the box earlier and had more time
to argue it all out. I see Jonquil's point of
view, of course, and feel in a way bound to
carry on for her sake, but—well, you know
my views about playing round with anything like magic and necromancy. Jonquil
says I'm morbid, still— Oh, well! come
and see us through it.*

RAFE.

May 27th, 1938.

I TRIED to pretend to myself that I
couldn't go, that I wouldn't go! But
even as I made these protestations inwardly,
I was giving instructions to the boy, Joe,
who daily and conscientiously thwarts my
best efforts to grow flowers, fruit and vege-
tables. For a quarter of an hour or so my
foredoomed struggle went on.

"——and Joe! that gallon of weed-killer
is for the whole lawn, don't pour it over
one dandelion root.

"It's merely one of his latest ideas, he
gets them like measles. I won't be fooled
into rushing off and leaving my garden
just now.

"Joe! if you let that dog bury his bones
in the new seedling-bed, I'll kill you when
I get back and bury you with them.

"All rubbish about his future! Another
few weeks would make all the difference
here! Why next Tuesday?

"Don't forget the quassia for the goose-
berries, Joe!

"——and what the devil has magic to do
with his future? No! I won't go! I won't
waste——"

By this time I was in the potting-shed,
kicking off my heavy shoes and scrambling
hastily into another and cleaner pair. Like
iron to a magnet, I was drawn to the house
where my mind continued to carry on acri-
monious debates while my body intelli-
gently took no notice of my mental dis-
turbance and obeyed my will.

I packed a bag, interviewed my old
housekeeper who expressed her disappro-
val of my plans by serving up watery
coffee and an India-rubber omelette for my
lunch, and set off within the hour with
parting instructions to expect me back in
God's good time.

It would have been more fitting to have
said in the devil's own time. So far, however, no tinge of the saturnine malice
which had, after a lapse of two centuries,

82

"Here is light for your sightless eyes."

begun to manifest itself, darkened the joyful anticipation of seeing my friend, Rafe Dewle.

I clambered into my old Austin-twelve and set her battered bonnet northwards. Those last hours on the open road when life was still free and untainted! Never, never again shall I experience anything like them. Knowledge has crippled imagination since then—evil polluted every spring of happiness.

On Shap Fells I stopped to cool my engine. Around me, yellow gorse breathed out its honey perfume; bumble-bees fussed to and fro as I lay stretched out on the heath and watched white cloud-feathers drift in the blue above. I slept for a brief spell on the warm breathing earth with the thin lonely call of curlews in my ears and the sense of hoary guardian hills all about me.

In sleep, the first faint brush of evil touched me. I dreamed that I journeyed on—on into a dark valley where, amidst mist and darkness and confusion, I felt the approach of invisible and threatening hosts. Yet I must go on swiftly—swiftly! Someone was waiting. Someone was in danger. I must hurry, hurry, hurry!

I woke to find my sunlit hemisphere all dark and angry. The great hills reared up threateningly into thunderous cloud-banks. Gusts of wind scattered the golden gorse-bloom and whistled the coming storm along over shivering grass and heather.

With a sense of urgent fear left by my dream I started my car and dropped by long winding loops of road down to the valley, and, as I tore along leafy green lanes toward Keswick this fear persisted. Once past the town, I drove even more quickly, cutting across the head of Borrowdale under dark Helvellyn's shadow and along the unfrequented road which led to *Braunfel*.

The rambling old manor house lay some twelve miles from town. I'd known it well when Rafe and I were boys together. His people had been wealthy landowners before 1914. The war took their men. The lean following years took their money and lands. *Braunfel* was on its last legs, financially, and I wondered why Rafe hadn't sold up before his marriage. I couldn't reconcile what little I knew of Jonquil French with the austere bare life that Rafe's inheritance offered. Their meeting and the marriage that so swiftly followed had been romantic and impassioned, a sort of Lochinvar affair; for Rafe had snatched her from another and very wealthy suitor almost at the church doors.

So characteristic of him and that hot Magyar blood of his! Even the lovely spoiled Jonquil French had succumbed to it. But for how long?

His letter indicated the thin end of a wedge to my mind. I'd met his bride in London and had not particularly liked her —not the wife for Rafe at all. I'd no idea what was the mysterious "thing" the pair disagreed about, of course, and I wished he'd been more explicit. Planning a good sensational story for me, no doubt. He loved being melodramatic.

At last I could see the bulk of *Braunfel* ahead, gray in shafts of pale clear light piercing a curtain of rain. About it, wide untended meadows stretched. Behind, the bare face of the fell, where only stumps remained of the great fir forest that had been so beautiful a background to the ancient house. War victims, those sheltering lovely trees! And no plantations showed their young green promise for the future. How gaunt *Braunfel* appeared! Not only that—it was positively sinister. I tried in vain to put the thought away. There was a look of boding grimness hanging over the massive pile that even neglected lands and bare scarred hillside could not wholly explain.

My old car splashed along the last mile

of muddy lane between high ragged hedges. The road turned and twisted like a sea-serpent. Preoccupied and depressed, I took a sharp angle and put on my brakes with a curse. A tall and very agile figure seemed to leap from right under the Austin's bonnet.

"Rafe! What the deuce——"

"Hello! Hello! you old mud-turtle! I forgive you—don't apologize!"

He opened the car-door, slid his long legs under the dashboard, put an arm about my shoulders and grinned in the old familiar way.

"You're a marvel, John. I didn't really count on your coming until tomorrow, but I got so restless thinking you might turn up that I've been hanging round for the last hour here. Never been so glad to see your solemn old mug in my life!"

My heart grew light at sight and sound of him. Marriage had not altered him as far as his friendship and affection were concerned; they were mine still, perfectly unchanged, the warmest, strongest tie I had in the world.

I grunted and glowered up at his face, dark as a gipsy's, lighted up with the inner fire that burned so strongly in him. I never knew man, woman, or child with so glowing, so intense a quality.

"Same old mad March hare!" I grumbled. "I'd hoped marriage might have given you a grain or two of sense. I suppose you realize you've practically ruined my garden for the next six months by dragging me up here?"

"Splendid! I have made a hero of you!"

He burst out into a wild barbaric song and yelled and yodeled until I drowned him with my car's horn. The noise was insane. We broke down and laughed like hyenas at last and I drove on feeling younger than I'd ever expected to feel again—my twenty-eight years had weighed heavily since Rafe's marriage.

SATURDAY, *May 28th*. Once under the steep gabled roofs of *Braunfel*, my bubble of delight was pricked. The sight of Jonquil French—Jonquil Dewle I should say—brought back the formless fear of my queer dream on Shap Fell. Why the sight of a girl like a princess in a fairy-tale should depress a man, I didn't know. Jealousy? No, neither of Rafe nor of his exquisite bride.

I had been jealous, afraid she'd come between us: I knew now most emphatically that she had not. Nor did I envy him. A woman has never yet roused the passionate thrill of joy I feel at sight of a perfect flower. It's no use arguing with me, I can't help it; that's the way I'm made.

"Mr. Fowler—John, I mean! How *perfect* that you've come! What a relief! You simply can't imagine what a time I've had lately. How lovely and large and shy you look! Isn't he *too* perfect, Rafe?"

"Certainly not. I refuse to live with two perfect beings. John's a mere man like myself."

She blew him a kiss, pirouetted round the dark paneled room like a little red flame blown on the wind, dropped on one knee before me and raised her hands in an attitude of prayer.

"Dear, dear John! You *are* perfect! Oh, if you could only see yourself. Just like a lovely solemn pine tree planted in the middle of our library. Please, please may I kiss you—I really must."

In a flash she was on her light dancing feet, her arms about me, her pleading face upraised. I bent a stiff reluctant head, received a moth-like touch on my lips and watched her and Rafe clasp each other in ecstatic amusement.

"I take it back, darling." Rafe wiped his eyes. "He certainly is—perfect."

"Well, now you've settled that, perhaps you'll start explaining things. You haven't brought me here to point out the singular beauty of my character?"

"No," chuckled Jonquil. "But you wouldn't be of any use to us unless you were such a perfect wise old owl."

Her smile glanced like sun on running water.

"Not time to explain before dinner. It's a long, sad tale. Rafe will take you up to your nice large drafty room, and when you hear a sound like a bull being massacred—come down for dinner. Rafe's invented a patent bugle-thing he uses when I'm late for meals; he's too lazy to walk the half-mile upstairs."

LEFT to myself in a bedroom whose size and dignity made me feel something like a small dry ham-sandwich on a platter designed for the traditional boar's head, I pushed open a diamond-paned lattice window, slumped down on the broad uncushioned seat beneath it and glared out at the cobbled garth below. Pigeons kept up a low bubbling complaint from roofs of stables and outbuildings—ruinous affairs, minus doors and windows, their slates and stones stained with centuries of rain, their woodwork gray and cracked, weeds, moss and lichen a green-gold signal of defeat.

It wasn't the garth, or the many evidences of poverty elsewhere that worried me, however, as I sat listening to the *broo! broo broo* of the pigeons. It was the thought of Jonquil.

It was impossible to do more than put into mere words her remarkable beauty, and what are words when it comes to a young, living, exquisitely made creature like her? She had crisp red-gold curls, eyes of changing deep warm brown that reminded me of wallflowers in sunlight, a milk-white skin, and body so light and quick in movement, so sure in poise, so extraordinarily expressive of her every mood that she seemed winged—a brilliant tropic bird darting and flashing to and fro.

But it was the will behind her laughing eyes that frightened me. Her will—blind, ignorant, unyielding, a terrible weapon in her reckless hands!

Abruptly, my dream possessed me again. . . . I was hurrying along that dark valley into mists and darkness and confusion—someone needed my help—I must hurry, hurry, hurry. And now Jonquil was beside me, her hand on my arm, her voice laughing, persuading, telling me to come back, come back, come back—she hindered me—I could not shake off her detaining hand. Her clear laugh prevented my hearing what my ears were straining for. I only knew I must hurry, hurry, hurry—in the gathering darkness ahead someone needed me. . . .

It wasn't until after leaving the dinner-table, graced no longer by Queen Anne silver and Waterford glass, that I realized the significance of Jonquil's inclusion in my disturbing and recurring dream.

Rain and wind turned the May night to chill discomfort. Rafe lighted the big library fire, piled up fir-cones and logs until a heartening blaze warmed a respectable area of the lofty room with its moldering books, threadbare rugs and worm-eaten oak.

Stimulated by tobacco, whisky, and Rafe's company I began to discount my boding fears again—but not for long. Jonquil was eager as Rafe seemed reluctant to enlighten me. He yielded to her importunity at last, lifted down an iron casket from a high bookshelf and set it on a heavy table near the fire.

"There you are, lady and gentleman!" he made an exaggerated showman's gesture. "This is the Luck of *Braunfel* and guaranteed to supply your heart's desire. To make its magic work you need a nice round full moon, a strong belief in ghosts and devils, and a bottle of my best whisky inside you. These will qualify you to commune with a Benevolent Gent who died two hundred years ago in the hope of an extraordinary Resurrection from the Dead."

His nonsense wasn't well received. The sight of that twelve-by-eight inch box filled me with a nasty crawling sensation of horror. I set down my glass and stared at it in silence.

Jonquil ran up to the table, tried to pull the box from beneath Rafe's long brown fingers.

"It's not fair—it's not fair to tell him like that! You're trying to prejudice him. Let *me* show him! Let *me* tell him!"

Instantly he became the bland infuriating nurse with a spoiled child, patted her shining coppery curls with one hand and imprisoned her impatient fingers with his other.

"Now! Now! Now! Remember there's a little visitor here, darling! Don't forget your pretty manners!"

He kissed and put her back in a chair with another admonitory pat on the head. "This is my Ancestor! My Benevolent Gent—hereafter known as B.G., and I will not be intimidated by a woman with red hair!"

I knew Rafe well. He was stalling now. It was a very old habit of his to approach anything he deeply disliked with idiotic badinage. Well, he might deceive Jonquil, but not me. So I sat tight and waited. My hands and feet grew cold in spite of the hot cheerful fire. I was most acutely awake, my eyes on Rafe's face, when that cursed dream of mine recurred . . . a dark long valley stretched between us . . . he faded, dissolved into distance and smoky dark confusion. . . .

"John! What is it?"

I FOUND myself on my feet, blinking stupidly down into Jonquil's alarmed face. Rafe was staring at me across the table, his mouth open in surprise.

"Cramp?" he inquired. "Must have been a bad twinge. I never heard you yell like that before."

"Cramp!" I echoed feebly, then pulled myself together. "No—it's a tooth—going to have it out."

I mumbled apologies, filled my glass, drank and felt considerably better. My mind cleared.

"Let's get down to business." I waved my pipe toward the box on the table. "I want to know where *I* come in. Let's have the story straight, mind!"

"John, you *are* such a darling! When you look at me like that through those enormous specs I feel just like a criminal before a judge."

Jonquil sat very stiffly and raised a hand as if to take an oath:

"I promise not to interrupt—unless I *have* to."

She tucked her little green slippers under her, curled up in the corner of a settee, and assumed an air of child-like innocent patience. I watched her with a pang. She was so sure of herself. She knew so exactly what she wanted—and intended to get it at all costs.

"Well?" my voice was brusk with anxiety as I turned to Rafe. "Bring out the skeleton in the cupboard."

His lips twisted in a rather doubtful smile.

"Queer you should say that. It's not exactly a skeleton, but it is part of a dead body."

"What? Your Ancestor, did you say— was he embalmed?"

"His heart was."

He lifted the casket's heavy lid as he spoke. A breath of thin cold air blew across my face and neck as I leaned forward to watch. I hated to see him standing over that beastly box; there was something so repulsive and ominous about it that my flesh crept when his fingers touched its rusty lid. Intuition told me that he did more than open a lid—he opened a door to something deadlier than plague.

It was a relief to my taut nerves to see him take out two tangible objects and set them on the table. One was a fat little book, fastened with broad brass clasps and bound in solid leather. The other— I got to my feet and went to examine it more closely.

My gorge rose at sight of the dark dried thing. I've seen mummies, and some were hideous enough. I've prowled about laboratories and examined scientific specimens preserved in fluids, and many were fairly revolting to a mind and imagination like mine. But this little horror, black and withered, with a strange metallic sheen! In amazement I drew still closer, unable to credit my sight. Then I straightened up with a jerk and glanced at Rafe.

"It's living! It beats—the thing beats!"

He nodded—"Since 1738, according to his tombstone date."

I saw he shared my revulsion. I forced myself to touch the heart, and drew back in horror at finding the dark withered bit of muscle was warm.

Jonquil clapped her hands. "You see! You see! Now perhaps you'll persuade Rafe to do it. Oh, he must—he must!"

She could contain herself no longer and flashed across to us. There wasn't a vestige of fear in her eager face as she put out a delicate exploring hand and touched the withered heart. Her faith in it, her strong will to test it, lent the dreadful thing power, and I saw it swell under her fingers —saw the throbbing pulse beat stronger, fuller.

"No! Don't!"

Rafe's voice sharply admonished her. His hand snatched back her own. She looked from him to me and laughed, but the red-brown eyes were bright with impatient anger.

"How exasperating men are! You look like two old hens with a duckling! I didn't think you'd be afraid to, John."

She gave me a stormy scornful glance. Next moment she was curled up in her corner again, sudden as a puff of wind.

"John, darling!" her voice was honey-sweet now; "that's a heart of gold. Quite literally a heart of gold for Rafe and me —if he chooses! Oh, I see what you're thinking. You're a sentimentalist like Rafe. I'm not. His heart won't reduce the Bank's overdraft, you know. That"— she flicked an airy hand toward the table— "that heart will."

I caught Rafe's glance at her and sharply realized his carefully concealed unhappiness. His shining tower of romance was fast changing to an old house in need of repair. The solitary countryside where he and she would walk in dreams was being reduced to an estate whose every hedge and gate and meadow clamored for money —money—money! I'd never felt the pinch of my own straitened circumstances before, but now I hated myself—I'd have given anything to put things right for Rafe. And I hated Jonquil too—unreasonably, fiercely, for making him unhappy.

I didn't answer her. I was watching Rafe as, with swift distasteful touch, he took up the repulsive little heart, restored it to its metal box and dropped the lid with a clang.

Then he picked up the squat leather book and I followed him to the fireside.

I was convinced he was as much relieved as I to have that beastly heart out of sight.

"Don't tremble in your shoes, old man! I'm not going to read this tome right through. It's full of queer stories and experiments that don't concern our problem directly. This is the really juicy bit that does."

He drew a stiff yellowed crackling sheet from a pocket of the book's cover and unfolded it with a flourish.

"This is the apple of discord in the house of Dewle! This is the bee in Jonquil's bonnet! This is what's muting the family lute! A scrap of paper—a thing capable of starting anything in the world

—wars, duels, murders—all the trouble that is, or ever will be."

"A check for £1,000,000 is a scrap of paper I'd love to see—with your name on it, dearest!"

"It was only £100,000 this morning," he reminded her. "Even a B. G. has limits, you must remember."

"And those that don't ask, don't get," she retorted with a flirt of her red curls.

"Well, we'll see what John thinks of my ancestor, Count Dul's *billet-doux*." He gave me a swift glance. "There's a preliminary but I'll spare you about his grave. It's been lost for generations, but Jonquil discovered it after reading this."

I could see the black thick lettering through the semi-transparent paper as Rafe held it up. He seemed to know it pretty well by heart, to judge by the way he galloped through the closely written lines:

This document concerns only those in whose veins my blood doth run, and who bear the ancient name of Dul. Let any such read these words with faith to believe and courage to obey, and to them will I grant the wish that lies most closely to their heart, be it for life beyond mortal span, for riches, for fame, or for the sweet delights of love. Let him who would seek my aid ask in the full knowledge that I, Count Dul, have power to give him his desire.

For his part, he must most strictly observe such instructions as are writ hereafter, failing not in any particular. Let him take careful heed therefore to obey.

THE DEED MUST BE DONE UPON A CERTAIN NIGHT and that the first night of a month of June when the moon is at the full between its second and third quarters.

I MUST BE SUMMONED BY ONE WHO STANDS BESIDE MY GRAVE and in such words as are graven upon the inner side of the Box in which this docu-

ment shall be discovered, together with the Book and my Heart.

AT THE FIRST LINE OF THE CONJURATION MY KINSMAN SHALL LIGHT A FLAME and it shall be of oil poured out in a black bowl and set at the foot of the grave.

AT THE SECOND LINE HE SHALL SPRINKLE EARTH UPON THE GRAVE and it shall be earth which fire has made bitter, and rain has washed, and the four winds blown upon.

AT THE THIRD LINE HE SHALL SET MY HEART AT THE HEAD OF THE GRAVE; then, kneeling beside it, he shall cut his left hand until his blood drops from it upon the heart.

LASTLY HE SHALL SUMMON ME IN A LOUD VOICE AND PRONOUNCE HIS WISH. And I shall hear him. And I will come to him. And whatsoever boon he asks, it shall be his.

RAFE stopped reading as abruptly as he'd begun, and held out the paper.

"You can read the Conjuration yourself. It's a bit melodramatic to declaim aloud just now."

I read in silence, then sat staring into the fire. The touch of the paper, its crabbed evil lettering and the hateful words themselves filled me with loathing.

"Well?" Rafe continued. "How's that for an ancestor? Jonquil's convinced that if I do my little song and dance he'll come rushing back from—well, this Book leaves no doubt from *where*—with a Present for a Good Boy under his ghostly arm."

"Yes, I'm convinced he would."

"Oh, John! You dear! You absolute darling!" cried Jonquil. "You *do* think there's something in it? You really and truly do! Oh, I'm thrilled. Rafe's been so exasperating about it. Now he'll simply *have* to give in."

"I didn't say that I agreed with you," I interrupted.

89

She sat up with a jerk, scattering cigarette ash over the satin iridescence of her dress. Black cold rage possessed me, brain and body. I knew I'd never make her understand—spoiled lovely little materialist that she was. Superstition urged her to snatch at this promised wealth. Ignorance blinded her to the hideous risk.

"You don't agree with me? You've just said you believed the Count could and would return!"

"Yes. I believe that."

"Well?" Her face grew radiant again. "Then you're just teasing! You *are* on my side, after all."

"No. Once and for all, I'm utterly against you. The man that wrote that promise and left behind him that foul thing"—I pointed to the box on the table—"must have been the devil's own brother."

"Oh-h-h!" wailed Jonquil. "You're not going to talk about demons and dangers and unholy powers, too! Rafe's been croaking like a raven for three whole days—and now you!"

"Go to it, old man!" urged Rafe. "She won't take it from me, but perhaps you can make her see it's not just money for jam."

I knew I couldn't move her, but I tried—explained, reasoned, argued, all to no purpose.

"It's no use trying to frighten me. You believe Count Dul can be brought back," she repeated for the twentieth time, "and that he could make Rafe a rich man. That's enough for me. He's only a ghost, poor thing! Perhaps he was just a harmless eccentric old man. Wouldn't make a will. Wanted to give it himself to his descendants."

"Harmless! What about that heart of his—beating two hundred years after his death? D'you think unaided human knowledge could leave *that* behind? Count Dul will surely return if the door is opened

to him. But it's forbidden. The dead may not—*must* not return."

"I can't see why not. You don't actually know any more than I do myself. You've read a lot of stuffy books and believe everything in them. I haven't. I'm unprejudiced. I'm willing to take risks."

"You mean to let Rafe take them."

Rafe, who'd sat listening with a queer twisted smile, laughed out at this.

"Hear! Hear! Exactly. Is *she* to do a pantomime scene at midnight by the grave of a disreputable old nobleman? No! Is *she* to chat with a two-hundred year old devil-worshipper in the moonlight? No! Is *she* asked to shed her good red blood on a thing that looks like a bit of cat's meat? No!"

"Well, Rafe, darling! It probably *is* all nonsense and I'm tired of arguing about it. Still——"

She jumped up from the settee and stood before the fire, facing the two of us.

"John has helped me, after all." She dropped me a mocking curtsy. "Yes, you dear old Solomon! You've helped enormously. Now I feel absolutely certain there *is* something in it, or you wouldn't be so worried.

"You know, darling," she turned to Rafe, "you promised to be guided by John's opinion. He's given it. He completely believes in your ancestor. And so do I—now! I'll never forgive you if you don't take a chance and try this thing out."

"Jonquil!" I was on my feet now, almost incoherent with fury. "What I believe in is the risk—the damnable risk of trying such a thing. You only believe in the money you want and shut your eyes to anything else. D'you suppose for a moment that dead Thing has waited two centuries to give you a fortune?"

She burst out laughing. "John, if you could only see yourself! You look like one of the Minor Prophets in action! There's a picture in the National Gallery that exactly——"

"Rafe!" I was almost shouting now. *"You* know enough, if she doesn't, to realize the wicked insanity of doing such a thing. D'you remember Harland and the sticky end he came to? And Browning who's gibbering away in an asylum? They happen to be men we know personally, but think of the hundreds of others who've been fools enough to think necromancy's a mere parlor game — who've deliberately walked into hell! It's hushed up—such cases always are. People are called mad, or reputed dead of heart attacks, etc. The truth is too beastly to publish."

"There's a good deal in what you say." Rafe had assumed a poise of amused detachment now. "I've not delved into occult lore as you have, old man. I dislike what I know, however. Still, Jonquil's attitude of 'nothing venture, nothing win' has a lot to recommend it."

She flew to him, took his hand in both her own.

"Oh! I knew, I *knew* you'd be an angel! You really mean to try it out?"

His answering look at her eager lovely face, his gesture as he rumpled her flaming aureole of hair, was sufficient for me. She'd won. My hot angry opposition had decided him, had pushed him into doing so. And I cursed myself for a pompous muddle-headed fool. I'd tilted the balance down—down to hell. If I'd kept calm and laughed at Count Dul, made light of the whole affair, Jonquil's belief might have faded. I'd lost my temper with her—lost my best chance by forcing Rafe to take her part. . . .

My dream enveloped me in its swirling vapor. . . . I was driving furiously down that long desolate valley—in the cloudy smothering darkness I heard a voice— *Count Dul! Count Dul! Count Dul!* The piercing cry was echoed by howls of laughter from the swirling mists—I drove on—

on — someone needed me — someone I loved, needed me. . . .

*S*UNDAY, MAY 29th. I spent a night of wretched anger and self-reproach and misery, interspersed with lapses into the haunting terror of my dream.

Rafe found me at eight a.m., empty pipe between my teeth, sitting on the stone parapet of a bridge, my thoughts dark and cold as the water I watched so gloomily.

"Not worth the usual penny, I can see!" Rafe came to perch beside me.

"Still, there's some excuse for you. Enough to make anyone broody—my estate! Reminds me of the hymn, 'Change and decay in all around I see'."

He patted me on the back.

"Cheer up, Jacko! And don't worry about the way things have turned out. This way—or another! What odds? I'm tremendously bucked up to have you here, and I'm bent on enjoying myself while I can. Forget Tuesday night—forget it! After all, you never know."

His look, his voice, his friendly touch cheered me. After all, as he said, one never *did* know! It was a relief to let myself be bluffed by his absurdly high spirits. Depression slipped off like a wet cloak as we tramped home for breakfast as carefree as if the pair of us had nothing more on our minds than a boat-race, or a thesis to be finished.

Jonquil appeared in high feather at the breakfast table—adorable with Rafe, mockingly sweet with me. And, of course, she scarcely talked of anything but Count Dul —how and when and where and what was going to happen about the wealth with which the family fortune was to be restored.

Rafe refused to be serious for even a moment about the B.G., as he called the Count. He was in the unreasoning fey mood that always seized him before any special test in our college days.

"I think the date's a mistake," he remarked. "The old boy meant April 1st."

I didn't remind him that the last night of May, this year, was peculiarly fitted for Count Dul's return. He knew considerably more than he acknowledged of ceremonial magic. It was unlikely that the significance of next Tuesday's date had escaped him. Together, as students, we'd read the Fourth Book of *Philosophia Occulta*, and the works of Pirus de Mirandola, and the *Grimoire* of Pope Honorius.

Above all, he'd read the book which Count Dul had left behind him. I'd borrowed and read it too, from cover to cover, and it was plain that Rafe's ancestor had, after many experimental essays, followed the teachings and practises of the infamous Lord of Corasse. These entailed observance of astronomy and, according to them, such a purpose as the return of the dead could only be accomplished at certain rare conjunctions of the stars and moon and planets. Rafe must be aware of these facts.

"Perhaps," Jonquil's face sparkled with excitement, "perhaps it will be priceless old jewelry he brought from Hungary. Count Dul was the first of your family to settle in England, wasn't he, Rafe?"

"He came because he was pushed," he replied. "They found he'd smuggled emeralds mined in the High Tatra Alps. He escaped from a particularly spectacular death connected with rope and four horses by a miracle—and, tradition records, by the aid of the devils he served."

"Emeralds!" breathed Jonquil, her eyes two deep pools of ecstasy. "How I adore emeralds! I shall keep the very most beautiful for myself, Rafe. You can sell the rest if I have just one perfect stone to wear."

"Certainly, Madam!"

He whipped out a notebook and pencil and assumed a business-like air.

"Let me see, now! What size and color does Madam prefer? I would not like to order something unsuitable. Oval, round, or square? Green or rose-red?"

"Rose-red," she took him up promptly. "A very very large square-cut stone set as a pendant with diamonds."

He licked his pencil and printed her order laboriously.

"You can take off that superior smirk, my child," he assured her. "There are such things as rose-red emeralds."

Their discussion went on to the end of the meal. Then she announced that we were all going to climb Hawes Fell.

"I've found a black bowl for the oil. All we need now is the earth."

"Earth! Climb up five hundred feet on a good Sabbath day of rest! Your breakfast has flown to your head, child. Think again—what about my untilled acres?"

"Doesn't it say the earth must be bitter with fire, and washed with rain, and blown on by the four winds? Very well, then. Wasn't there a heath-fire on Hawes Fell last month? It's as black as soot now and soaked in rain, and every wind in the world blows up there."

She'd made up her mind. It was to be earth from Hawes Fell, and the remainder of the day was spent in getting it.

TUESDAY NIGHT, MAY 31st. Tuesday morning—afternoon—night. At last, Tuesday night.

Rafe and I stood waiting for Jonquil in the library. It was after eleven p.m. In a few minutes we should set out across the fields to where Count Dul's grave lay. From the Book he'd left it was clear that in England, as in his own native country, the Count had been excommunicated by the Church and his body buried therefore in unconsecrated ground. It was Jonquil's indefatigable curiosity that had discovered the grave with its broken headstone in one of Rafe's outlying meadows. It was this initial discovery that had first determined her to carry out the remainder of the Book's instructions.

"Who actually found the metal box?" I asked now.

The constraint between Rafe and myself on this last day had made me desperate. He'd steadily avoided being alone with me until now, although I'd persistently sought such opportunity, for today Jonquil had, for the first time, weakened in her project. Too obstinately proud to say outright she was afraid, she'd endeavored in round-about ways to get Rafe to change his mind. He'd refused to rise to her bait, brushed aside her every tentative move toward canceling the date he'd determined to keep with his B.G.

But her wavering had given me a gleam of hope. Perhaps I might persuade him out of his insanely dangerous rendezvous even now. I felt sure Jonquil had given me this last chance to do so.

"Was it you who found the box?" I repeated.

He gave me a queer slanting look, half speculative, half sad.

"It found me," he laughed. "Slipped from the top of a bookshelf. I haven't the slightest recollection of seeing it in the house before. Never heard my father mention it. Must have been pushed out of sight somehow—it fell with a crash right at my feet and the Book and the B.G.'s heart rolled on the floor."

"Rafe! Don't go on with this. Even Jonquil doesn't want it now. You know —you surely know the risk. Why will you——"

He caught my eye, and changed color. I saw he was trying to bring himself to answer me, and waited. He began to speak in quick, almost stammering words.

"Yes, I know the risk. I know, old man, but—I must go on now. It's been heaven —these last six months with Jonquil— heaven! But it can't last. We married in haste, but I'm damned if I'll let her 're-

pent at leisure.' It's a million to one I'll come through—with money, or without it, tonight, but—she'll remember I've tried."

"Rafe! You can't . . . you won't——"

"I will. It's easier to die than to lose her. I can face any hell but that."

"But she's going to—to lose you. And she's afraid of that now. She'd be glad— thankful if you gave up."

He smiled, as he'd smiled a thousand times when I'd missed some obvious point.

"Dear old chap! You don't know Jonquil. She's temperamental—just working up to the proper goose-flesh mood for tonight's orgy. No use, John! I'd never live it down if I failed her now. She's a child, an adorable child. I've had more than most men—and I'm choosing the easiest way out."

Jonquil's light step sounded on the uncarpeted old stairway.

"Ready?" her shining curls appeared round the door. "It's after eleven o'clock. We ought to start."

We went out to the great, echoing hall; our feet, on the old-fashioned red tiles, clanked dismally.

"This the picnic basket?" Rafe took up Count Dul's box from an oak chest. "Got the champagne and oysters, dear? Right! Let's start."

THE night was cool, almost cold. Wind stirred in the tree-tops. Tall solemn elms on either side of the avenue whispered uneasily as we passed between their double ranks. Overhead a brilliant sky of stars, and a proud moon sailing in full majesty.

I wondered if any remote world up there was like the one I trod; if any other beings knew such bitterness and horror and evil as we did on our earth. I wondered if I could go on living here — alone, when Rafe—when Rafe——

Suddenly my dream blotted out moon, stars, and earth. . . . I had reached the end of that awful valley — breathless, spent from long pursuit—before me a broken pathway descended to the lip of a yawning chasm. And along that path, walking with steady purposeful tread, a man's tall figure loomed. Rafe—it was Rafe! In agony I stumbled after him. . . .

My dream blew like mist from across my vision. I was back in a country lane with Rafe and Jonquil, under the full moon's menace, the moon that would presently light Count Dul from hell.

"Here's our field-path." Jonquil turned aside to an old stile of flat stones laid with gaps between to keep cattle from crossing.

We followed her, cut across a field to another stile and across it to the desolate overgrown rocky bit of wasteland that was our objective. In another minute Jonquil stopped and pointed.

"There! There it is!"

The white merciless moon showed up every grass-blade and flower and stone of the hummock before us. Nature had flung a poisonous pall over the dead, and even the moon's glare could not blanch the blotched evil of henbane, viper's bugloss and deadly nightshade, or the scarlet-spotted fungus on Count Dul's grave. A cracked and sunken headstone leaned awry at the head of it. The worn lettering showed only a few words of whatever inscription had been cut two hundred years ago—COUNT DUL . . . DIED 1738 . . . A WARNING TO ALL WHO READ . . .

Rafe looked at his watch, glanced up at the moon as it climbed to its fateful meridian. He'd doffed his armor once more. With mocking brilliant smile he looked down on the horrible grave and airily kissed his hand.

"Rafe!" Jonquil's brows went up in anxiety. "You *must* be serious."

"Darling! I'm sure the B.G. wouldn't like it. Think what a gay old dog he was

in his time. Think how much he must have enjoyed himself to have tried for two centuries to get back again. Must make his little trip enjoyable, you know! About time I got to the front door to meet him. I suppose it's no use arguing any more— you won't go home?"

"For the hundredth time—no, dearest! You might take my rose-red emerald and run off with some other pretty lady."

She was looking up into my face and, even to my jaundiced eyes, was a sight to stir the blood of any man. For a second, Rafe's devil-may-care mask dropped, his dark burning eyes and drawn features showed such anguish that I started forward with a cry. This was my dream . . . his tall figure—so dear, so obstinate, so tragic — moving steadily onward to the edge of an abyss. . . .

At once he recovered himself. Behind the brilliant smile he turned to me I read entreaty. He wanted me to take Jonquil away. He was in terror of what she would see and hear, in terror that she might be endangered too. But I knew also, and it was the only poor comfort I had left, that he wanted me—needed me as he and I always needed each other in a tight corner.

No one on earth—nor from hell— should move me from that graveside, and I confess I was glad that Jonquil should be there also. I wanted to spare her nothing.

I hoped if Rafe did not survive that she too would be destroyed.

I don't know how much of my thoughts he read, but in any case she wouldn't have left with me. He turned away, opened the metal casket, lifted out of it the withered pulsing heart and set it down at the head of the grave under the deeply sunken headstone.

My fascinated gaze was held by the horrible little thing. I saw it throb and quiver to the beat—beat—beat of whatever infernal power quickened life in it. I saw its dark withered walls gleam in the moonlight like tarnished copper.

At the other end of the grave, Rafe uprooted a clump of spotted henbane, set down a small black bowl and poured oil into it.

Jonquil's small hands clasped in excitement. She watched with dancing eyes, her curls ruffled about her eager flower-like face.

Rafe glanced at his watch again, smiled once more at Jonquil. He didn't look toward me—I was thankful for it.

"Now for my old B.G. Stand back! Stand back, there!" he waved an imperious hand. "Make way for the Count Dul— make way———"

He took from his pocket the crackling parchment on which the conjuration was written, its black lettering very plain in the moonlight, ran his eye over it for the last time, although I was certain every word of it was stamped deep in his memory.

His voice rang out as I'd heard it ring on the playing-fields when we were boys together:

For your sightless eyes—this Flame!

He stooped to set alight the oil in the black bowl.

For your fleshless bones—this Earth!

He scattered dry dark soil from the basket.

For your withered heart—this Blood!

He knelt, held out his left hand and slashed it with a knife until blood dripped upon the heart. Then he got swiftly to his feet. His loud voice challenged the dead:

Wake from your sleep, Count Dul!
Rise from your grave, Count Dul!
Return from the dead, Count Dul!
Give me wealth—wealth for my boon!

My body was turned to ice, my feet rooted to the ground, my whole being concentrated on Rafe's tall rigid figure standing at the graveside—at the mouth of hell.

His last word echoed and reverberated like an organ-note; louder — louder it

swelled and boomed, until the quiet night hummed and quivered, and the poisonous grave-weeds slowly withered, blackened, lay in dust, until the earth beneath them cracked widely open and the burning oil shot up into a red roaring fire that was cold as wind off an ice-field and seemed to lick the stars.

It froze the tears on my cheek. It chilled even the unbearable anguish in my heart.

The heart—in the red flame's brilliance —shone, incandescent, fiercely alive, then vanished.

In that moment the flame sank to earth again, the noise of its burning ceased—silence far more ominous fell, while overhead the great moon looked down in passionless survey.

The grave yawned widely open; from its void rose a wisp of dark smoke that turned and wreathed and twisted and coiled in ever denser volume as it swelled and blew and eddied to and fro above the gaping grave, blind, purposeless, uncertain. Then a nucleus formed in the vaporous evil, a dull purplish-red heart-shaped glowing core about which the dark mist swiftly formed and re-formed to a tall swaying pillar—an imperceptibly growing outline —a recognizable human body whose white face of damnation stared into Rafe's, whose awful rotted hands reached out to touch. to hold, to bind him fast.

And now I could not distinguish Rafe from the smothering infernal Thing itself. It swirled about him. It covered head and hands and feet from sight. When he moved, he moved within the enveloping darkness. When his face turned to me I saw only the dreadful livid face of the dead.

Still I was frozen there, unable to speak, to move, to do more than see and hear the Thing that now moved forward with fixed pale staring eyes and loose dark lips that mouthed and laughed and whispered as it came.

I could not turn to look at Jonquil. I felt her arms about me, clutching—I felt her warm soft body pressed to mine, her face against my cold and empty heart. I heard her long shrieks echoing above the thin dry whisper of the Thing that steadily advanced—nearer—nearer.

It halted beside us. Now I could see Rafe's tortured eyes, his face and form behind the clouded horror that enfolded him—he was shut up inside it like a chrysalis in a dark cocoon. He was Count Dul —Count Dul was Rafe!

Next moment Jonquil was plucked from my side. Her body was flung down on the dew-wet earth, her curls gleamed as two hands met about her throat, choking a last thin cry. . . .

The Thing that killed her rose and moved back to the grave. Now I could see Rafe more distinctly beneath the wavering cloud of evil. His dreadful garment grew thin and patchy, drifted from him, lost density and outline as it hovered over the open grave.

And the grave's darkness sucked it down out of sight, back to the hell from which it came.

The yawning hole closed up. The ugly weeds grew rank again upon the hummock. A sunken headstone leaned awry at its end.

In the same moment, I was released and ran stumbling over the long grass to where Rafe lay huddled.

A MONTH later. Rafe was not dead. But he would have died—he *would* have died if that devil hadn't barred his way out!

By some infernal miracle, and after lying unconscious for a week, Rafe woke to full possession of his faculties. No memory was spared him of that fatal resurrection, or of Jonquil's unthinkable end.

He lives to remember it hour after hour, day after day, week after week.

For another two months his torture will endure. Then he will be hanged. That much is certain. He confessed to the murder of his wife and stands trial next week. He'll plead guilty and there'll be practically no defense. Neither he nor I mean to confess a word of the actual truth. It would condemn him to years and years of life as a criminal maniac—remembering —remembering. . . .

A murderer—and a millionaire! Oh, yes! Count Dul kept his promise. A will turned up when the Chief Inspector of Police was going through Rafe's papers in the library—the thing toppled off a bookcase at the inspector's feet. It stated that the count had left a legacy buried in the cellars of *Braunfel*.

The police dug it up. Emeralds! An astounding collection which was photographed and written up in every rag in the country.

The finest gem was a great rose-red emerald, cut square and set with diamonds as a pendant.

I burned the Book and the Conjuration. I threw the metal box into Lake Derwentwater. But I couldn't find the heart—I went over every inch of the grave and all round about it.

Rafe takes this as a sign Count Dul's power is expended. I'm thankful that he doesn't understand.

I know that devil will return somehow —somewhere! Jonquil's death means life for him. Her will to live is added to his own.

When Rafe dies, he will look for her— and never find her. Never. She is one with the Count now, part of his thought, his will, his enduring evil.

Whether I can learn his secret, learn enough to meet him—and destroy him— I don't yet know.

When I am left alone, it will be all that remains worth doing in a world of fear and shadows.

www.ingramcontent.com/pod-product-compliance
Lightning Source LLC
Chambersburg PA
CBHW030537180626
46810CB00005B/1914